Accla
Mi<

"Michael Lister may be the author of the most unique series running in mystery fiction. *The Body and the Blood* proves that once again. It crackles with tension and authenticity." —Michael Connelly

"Lister, a real-life prison chaplain who knows his turf, delivers gritty portrayals of inmates and prison workers." —*Publisher's Weekly*

"Lister's descriptions of a prison setting, as well as the situations Jordan encounters, are about as real as it gets—and it's not surprising. *Power in the Blood* is the first novel for the North Florida resident who spends his days working as a chaplain for the Florida Department of Corrections." —*Orlando Sentinel*

"*Power in the Blood* is a first novel that takes a uniquely uncompromising view of grace." —*Kirkus Reviews*

"Michael Lister, a North Florida prison chaplain, is a first-time author, but you'd never know it. His novel, *Power in the Blood*, reads like it was dreamed up by a skillful old pro. The cruel, small world inside prison could make for an unpredictable, claustrophobic series. Something untried, different, interesting. Thank heaven."
—By Connie Ogle, *The Miami Herald*

"A realistic drama and surprising character depth. The spiritual dimension of John's inner life adds a depth that's often absent in the mystery genre. A realistically portrayed prison setting and a cast of characters depicted with complexity and nuance together form a quietly effective character-study/whodunit."
—*Kirkus Reviews starred review*

"Author Michael Lister perfectly blends religion into a gritty, realistic look at prison life without preaching or overpowering his solid plot. Lister invigorates the religion mystery inside a hard-boiled novel."
—Oline Cogdill, *South Florida Sun Sentinel*

"*Blood of The Lamb* is a gripping locked-room murder mystery. Unflinchingly brutal in its portrayal of violence, sexual abuse, and murder within the prison setting, Blood of the Lamb comes alive with chilling reality and fully humanized, believable character portraits all the way up to the end. Highly recommended for mystery fans for its attention to detail and lack of questionable contrivance."

—*Midwest Book Review*

"Michael Lister proved his worth as a writer with his first book, *Power in the Blood*. He's done it again with his second John Jordan mystery, *Blood of the Lamb*. There are more sinners than saints in this tautly written mystery. Readers will find themselves sympathetic to Jordan, a man with troubles of his own whose conscience won't allow him to accept a cover-up by prison authorities. Highly recommended." —*Mystery Scene Magazine*

"Michael Lister is a genius at evoking the dangerous mood of a prison while, at the same time, showing how the light of redemption shines even in the darkest places. *Blood of the Lamb* is tense and tightly plotted, a true page-turner until the very satisfying ending."

—Margaret Coel

"These seven stories featuring complex and engaging Florida prison chaplain Jordan represent various suspense and puzzle-spinning approaches, but the most memorable are centered on theological mysteries: a nun who is medically declared both pregnant and a virgin; a 10-year-old Hurricane Katrina refugee who claims to be Jesus Christ; and a consideration of the pros and cons of the Shroud of Turin. Margaret Coel, whose own novels feature a painfully chaste relationship somewhat similar to Jordan's with a prison coworker, provides an introduction. —*Ellerry Queen Mystery Magazine*

"Stylish, retro, and highly entertaining, Michael Lister's PI Jimmy "Soldier" Riley is a compelling new noir hero." —Jason Starr

"A seductive mix of sudden violence and raw emotion, Michael Lister's *The Big Goodbye* is a much-welcome contribution to the hardboiled, P.I. tradition. Cool stuff." —Victor Gischler

Another Quiet Night in Desperation

Desperation

The Florida Noir Series

www.FloridaNoir.com

also by the author

The John Jordan Series
Power in the Blood
Blood of the Lamb
Flesh and Blood
The Body and the Blood
Blood Sacrifice
Rivers to Blood

Florida Noir
Another Quiet Night in Desperation
The Jimmy "Soldier" Riley Series
North Florida Noir
The Big Goodbye

Another Quiet Night in Desperation

stories

Michael Lister

Pottersville Press
Panama City, Florida

Copyright © 2008 by Michael Lister

All rights reserved. No part of this book may be reproduced in any form or by any means, electronic or mechanical, including photocopying, recording, or by any information storage and retrieval system, without permission in writing from the publisher.

This book is a work of fiction. Any similarities to actual incidents, places, or people, living or dead, are entirely coincidental.

Inquiries should be addressed to:
Pottersville Press
P.O. Box 35038
Panama City, FL 32412

Lister, Michael.
    Another Quiet Night In Desperation/Michael Lister.
Florida - Fiction
-----1st ed.
      p.   cm.
   ISBN (10) 1-888-146-20-6
   ISBN (13) 978-1-888146-20-2

First Edition

Printed in the United States

Design by Adam Ake

For Lynn Wallace

Author's Note

Reader beware!

You're about to travel into another dimension—a dimension not only of sight and sound but of mind. By turning the page you're committing to taking a dark journey into a noirish land whose boundaries are that of the shadowed imagination. That's a signpost up ahead. Your next stop: Desperation!

The cruel, claustrophobic town of Desperation isn't exactly a vacation destination, but I love returning to it time and again. I've always liked the dark—especially in film and literature. To me, there's no better place to explore our devils and angels than in art. I enjoy seeing characters in difficult circumstances, desperate situations. It's in a caldron that true character is revealed.

But Desperation isn't for everyone—and not only because of the grittiness.

This disparate collection of stories includes not only crime, violence, betrayal, and revenge, but graphic sexuality (the last particularly strong in *Janie's Got a Gun, Pillow Talk, and The Day of Undoing*). Like every other facet of these tales, I think the sexual content is vital to the story, as essential as all other elements—without it, the stories aren't true, aren't what they were meant to be.

I've been questioned about the inclusion of the more sexually graphic stories in this collection—especially *Pillow Talk* and *The Day of Undoing*. The concern is that readers drawn to the crime stories might find the stories of shadowy sexuality off-putting. But noir has always been fascinated with the darker side of sexuality, and the unifying theme of this collection is not crime, but desperation—the town and the condition—whether it's down a mean street, in a by-the-hour motel, or on a marital bed.

I hope you'll still turn the page and take the journey, but won't hold it against you if you decide not to; either way—

You've been warned.

Contents

Introduction	11
Another Quiet Night in Desperation	15
Bait and Switch	29
Trapped	47
Janie's Got a Gun	63
The Exchange	89
Pillow Talk	97
The Day of Undoing	105
Tables	113
The Hunt	117
Barely Legal	135
Making Amends	159
Death of a Desperate Woman	181
Acknowledgments	199

Introduction
by Jim Pascoe

Yeah, it's true. I'm quite familiar with desperation. I mean, come on. I live in Hollywood.

No, not Hollywood, Florida, which is a real city; unlike my neighborhood in Los Angeles, which exists on signs and shows and movies but is really more a state of mind. So for those of you who have never been out this way and only know Hollywood from what you see on TV, let me break it down for you:

Hollywood is a slum.

Sure, it's in a bit of an upswing. The Academy Awards are actually held here again and not in some Masonic lodge downtown. Hot spot bars are sprouting up faster than arsonists — excuse me, I mean "accidents" — can burn them back down. But don't let the gentrification fool you. The dark parts are still dark. And the ugly — yeah, it's still ugly.

There's a reason I'm mentioning all of this, and it's because when I first visited Michael Lister for the Gulf Coast Writers Conference, I felt an instant kinship both with him as a writer and with the eerie beauty of North Florida. In fact, I became practically obsessed with the old paper mill towns like Port St. Joe, like Destin, like Desperation.

Desperation, just like Hollywood, is a slum. I don't mean this as a casual put down. Look beneath the surface; that's right, it's dirty, the worst kind of dirty, the dirty from the dirt of broken dreams. It's a landscape that's quiet, too quiet. When I was there and closed my eyes, I could hear secrets whistling through the thin paper trees.

Michael Lister must have heard them too ... only when he opened his eyes, he put the voices on paper. He captured their pain, their longing, their desires, their guilt, their desperation. That's noir, baby. It screams through this collection. Not in some kind of punk, pulpy throwback. No private dicks in fedoras. No venetian blinds. No rat-a-tat-tat. The noir of these stories comes from people making bad decisions, from mistaken observations, from the downward spiral of lost souls.

What I love most in these pages is the sense of doom that drips over everything. There is never doubt that bad shit is going to happen. You don't know when it's going down — hell, you might not even get to see it go down — but, believe me, it is going to go down.

At its best, this gives each story an urgency, one that makes me want to skip ahead because I have to find out what happens next. Whether it's simple lines like this classic from "The Hunt":

> His phone rang again. It never
> rang, and now it had rung twice
> in the last few minutes.

Or this delicious dialog exchange from "Bait and Switch" in which a mysterious creep asks a young computer wiz to do him a simple job. In Desperation, nothing is simple, and as the job drags on, the boy asks...

> How long we gonna do this?
> Not long, he said. It won't take long.
> What won't?

Let me tell you, a wicked smile comes across my face every time I read this. As a writer, I try to achieve this same quality of uncertainty and tension with all my work. It's rarely easy, though when a writer succeeds, it seems simple and effortless.

In *Another Quiet Night in Desperation*, Michael Lister succeeds.

So enjoy these dark tales. I'll see you again, right around the corner.

Jim Pascoe
Hollywood, California
May, 2008

Another Quiet Night in Desperation

Thoreau said most men lead lives of quiet desperation and go to the grave with the song still in them. He must have lived in a town like Desperation—a desolate little mill town in North Florida where the leading cause of death is boredom.

Thoreau's quote haunts me—especially on nights like tonight when Dita's working late at the school and I'm sitting on an uncomfortable barstool in Eddie's sipping on Hurricanes, which Eddie makes with genuine Florida key limes (not the Persian ones most growers switched to after the hurricane of 1926 wiped out their crops).

Randy Thomas, Eddie says, considering me. That your first and last name or is Thomas your first name and you're a horny bastard?

I smile. It's not the first time I've heard that, but I don't mention it.

It's a weeknight, and Eddie's is nearly empty. I'm sitting alone at the bar, which is the way I like it. It's easier to ponder Thoreau and shit when you don't have some rum-dumb slobbering in your ear.

As I finish my drink, Eddie looks at me, and I nod.

Mix me up another of your perfect storms, I say.

You sure? he asks.

You hear any ambivalence in my voice?

No, but hurricane season hasn't started yet, so you may want to—

I seem impaired to you?

Eddie holds his hands up, palms out. Okay. Okay. You're not ambivalent and you're not impaired.

I'm not a very patient motherfucker either, I say, but smile to take the edge off of it.

Eddie's okay, if a little conscientious for a barkeep. Like his establishment, he's small, serviceable, and dark. At times he acts as though he's compensating for something—perhaps his diminutive size, but only occasionally, and he's never been anything but nice to me.

Coming right up, he says. Who shall we name this one on after?

How about Cecilia?

Who is?

Just a girl I used to know, I say.

You've already used a 'C.' Remember? How about Dita?

Dita, my wife of three years, still hasn't forgiven me for moving her from New York, where our careers were just beginning to gain some traction, to this little backwoods, smoke-filled town that smells perpetually of rotten eggs. But like so many people in mill towns, my mom had cancer and needed us to take care of her. Dita and I temporarily gave up acting and play writing to teach English and drama at Desperation High. I say temporarily, but Mom died a while back and we're still here.

I shake my head. She doesn't blow like she once did, I say.

What married woman does? he says. She workin' late *again*?

I know what he's implying, but I act as if I don't. By far the sexiest woman in town, Dita is believed by the bored, desperate locals to be too hot not to be making the rounds.

Dita has an academic advisory meeting at the school, after which she is going to her classroom to grade papers—or so she says. I suspect she is secretly working on a new play.

Lot of papers to grade, I say, then take a sip of the new drink he sets down in front of me. And she's working with a bunch of kids who speak English as a second language.

He gives me a confused look. I didn't think we had many—

Redneck's their first.

Seems I recall that's what you spoke before you moved off to New York City and got all Yankified.

I smile. There's no one in New York who would confuse me for one of their own.

I don't suppose your knock on our little town includes Nathan, does it? he asks.

Nathan Adams, the one bright spot in my otherwise bleak existence here, is a talented, earnest young actor with a commitment to craft in his heart rather than stars in his eyes. Though he's far more talented than I'll ever be and there's not much I can teach him, I tell myself I'm staying in Desperation for him. My plan is to stay just until the end of this school year when he graduates, making my escape when he leaves for college.

No, he sounds like a hick, too, I say. You can't grow up in this town and not, but he just *sounds* like one.

He shakes his head to himself, his mouth forming something between a frown and a smirk. I've insulted his home and his people—and it doesn't matter that I've done it as an insider who grew up here.

If you despise Desperation so much, why're you still here?

It's a good question, one I ask myself all the time. Thing is, Thoreau never said how to get out.

People say you stay for Nathan, he says.

I raise my eyebrows and motion for him to elaborate.

Say you guys are too close for a teacher and student.

So New York turned me Yank and gay?

He shrugs. Just telling you what the talk of the town is. Not saying I believe it.

I stand, a little unsteadily, gripping the edge of the bar for support. Just looking out for me, huh?

He nods.

I drop another twenty on the bar. Not afraid of losing my business?

No gay bars in Desperation, he says. Where you gonna go?

It's a quiet night in Desperation. The setting sun suffuses downtown with a golden glow that makes the old buildings look better than they should. It's magic hour, that short span of perfect lighting during which Hollywood directors love to roll their cameras—no harsh illumination, no deep shadows, a graceful light that covers a multitude of blemishes.

I smile to myself at the town talk. I've become an outsider here. I'm not gay, and I doubt Nathan is, though I can't deny we have a certain connection, a certain attraction. Dita's not sleeping around, though I can't deny she's as unhappy as I am.

I stumble through downtown slowly, carefully, trying not to fall or attract attention to myself. The short, narrow Main Street of the business district, like the shops that border it, is empty. The lights are off in the small gift boutiques, closed signs hang in the windows of the deli, the bakery, and the fishing tackle store.

Sometimes when I drink too much, I get the same aura as when I'm about to get a migraine, and right now I can't tell which it is. I can only hope the way I'm feeling is from my own little hurricane season.

Walking helps, and by the time I reach my car, I'm a bit more steady, if not quite sober. I drive to the school. The front parking lot is filled with the vehicles of the parents and teachers attending the academic advisement meeting. Dita's lime green Bug is among them. I pull around back and park behind the theater lab. I'm not sure why I'm here. I left Eddie's earlier than I had planned and now find myself at a loss.

Unsteadily unlocking the door, I stumble into the large black box of the lab and flip on a single stage light. Making my way down to the front, I climb up on the stage, realizing how much I've missed it. Watching kids perform the techniques you've taught them, is not the same as performing yourself, and I long to once again strut and fret my hour upon the stage.

The play is the thing, I say aloud, and my words quickly soak into the absorptive material. All the world's a stage, I add, a little louder this time, but my words still die a quick death.

With my back to an imaginary audience, I turn quickly and, in that brief spin, begin to embody the greatest character ever created for the stage.

To be or not to be? I ask earnestly.

The turn was a bad idea, and it feels as if the room is still spinning around me, but I gather myself and continue.

That is the question. Whether tis nobler in the mind to suffer the slings and arrows of outrageous fortune or to take arms against a sea of troubles and by opposing, end them. To die, to sleep—no more, and by a sleep to say we end the heartache and thousand natural shocks that flesh is heir to. Tis a—

I'm startled to see Dita sitting on the front row watching me. I didn't even see her come in. Was I that immersed in the roll?

Get thee to a nunnery, I tell her, but in the fraction of a moment it takes me to blink, she's no longer there.

I rub my eyes and look again. She is gone. Actually, she was never there.

Shaking my head, I step to the front of the low stage and collapse.

For a while, I just sit in the dark, empty box, letting my mind wander. It doesn't take long before the heaviness in my head settles onto my chest and I find it difficult to breathe. Until this moment, I have believed myself to be bored, but now I think it may be depression I'm battling, that old small-town, environmental kind that comes from the space, pace, and silence to actually hear what's going on inside you.

I need to get out of my head, but I'm not sure how. I don't feel as though I can move, but then the phone rings.

I fumble with it a moment, then finally get it to my ear.

It's Nathan. Evidently he's at least bi, because a girl he's been fooling around with is dead and he needs my help.

I walk through the dark hallways of Desperation High, recalling how much I hated high school and how I swore I'd never be back—not for homecomings, not for class reunions, not for love or money—yet here I am. Careful to avoid the crowd in the commons, I meander around the back way. Still, within four minutes of receiving Nate's call, I'm entering the boys' locker room in the gym.

The locker room smells much the way it did back when I was a student here—layer upon layer of boys' basest bodily orders mixed with a tinge of ineffectual cleaning chemicals.

Block walls and vinyl composition tile floors, the locker room has showers and bathroom stalls on one long wall and a row of lockers on the other. The two short walls on each end have a single door in them—one exterior, the other an interior that opens into the gym.

The lockers sit on a long block shelf covered in the same vinyl the floor is and has a ledge that extends outward far enough to be used as a seat. Nathan is sitting on it, staring down at the bizarre spectacle at his feet. There on the floor, in part of the school's bulldog mascot costume, an American flag, and a couple of old basketball jerseys—all of which are wrapped in massive amounts of white athletic tape—a body like a roll of carpet lies at his feet.

Nate, I say.

He raises his head very slowly and looks up at me, but he doesn't say anything.

You okay? I ask, the inanity of my question dawning on me only after I pose it.

Not really, he says.

What happened?

I'm not sure, he says. We were about to fool around a little. We hadn't even done anything yet. I mean, we were kissing and all, but that's it. I went to the bathroom. When I got back she wasn't breathing.

You call an ambulance?

I should have, he says, but I just panicked. I gave her CPR for a few minutes, but nothing I tried worked. She was gone, and by the time I realized there was nothing I could do for her, it was too late for anyone to do anything—probably was even when I came back in here and found her. I found a little bracelet thing in her purse that said she had a heart condition.

Who is it?

New girl, he says. Name's Megan.

What exactly do you want me to do?

Help me take her home, he says. That's where she's supposed to be. Her parents are in the academic advisory meeting in the commons.

So's Dita.

We could sneak her in her room.

They'll do an autopsy, I say.

She died of natural causes, Randy. I swear.

When a student calls you by your first name, it's probably a sign the relationship has become inappropriate. Of course, if you're about to help him move a dead body it's probably not something to get hung up on.

I didn't know who else to call.

It's okay, I say. I'm glad you—

Just then someone jerks on the interior door and I jump. We both freeze.

It's okay, Nathan whispers. It's locked. It's probably the cleaning lady.

You don't think she has a key? I whisper back.

I blocked it.

Then she'll come around to the other door. We've gotta get out of here. As soon as the meeting is over, the whole school will be swarming with people. You got all your stuff?

As he begins to gather his things, I look around the locker area and then step into the bathroom, hoping not to see anything that makes me regret what I'm doing anymore than I already do.

Ready? Nathan asks.

What about *her* things?

They're wrapped up in there with her.

I see myself in the cloudy mirror and pause for a moment. I look older than my thirty-two years—pale-skinned, dark-eyed, depressed. Why hadn't I noticed it before? I'm depressed. It's a relief actually. I might be able to do something about it.

I shake my head and look away. That's when I see it—traces of blood in one of the sinks, but I don't say anything. It's a locker room. Several hundred kids come through here every day. I tell myself somebody could've gotten hurt in PE, but I don't believe it.

Still, something like this would ruin his life, and I can't let that happen. Maybe if I weren't so depressed, hadn't had so many Hurricanes, I'd feel differently—or feel something at all, but as it is I'm just gonna ride this one out, see where this dark detour leads. Of course, maybe it's not depression or intoxication at all. Maybe I care more for Nate than I've admitted to myself.

The body is heavier than I expect.

We carry it like a roll of carpet through the dark hallway on the back side of the school. I've chosen this route because it avoids the commons and all the potential witnesses it holds, and because the security camera covering this area hasn't worked for months.

The hallway is circular, the library on the inside, classroom doors lining the outside, and we can only see a about ten feet in front of us at any given time.

Up ahead, I hear footsteps and the jangle of keys. As I quickly reverse my steps, Nathan is caught off-guard and drops the body, which makes a muffled thud as it hits the floor.

Somebody's coming, I whisper. Come on.

He grabs the body and we duck into a small alcove next to two closed and likely locked classroom doors. And wait.

My heart is pounding so hard, my shirt flutters above my chest.

Why am I doing this? I wonder again. The real answer comes immediately, and I'm surprised I haven't thought of it before.

Dita and I can't have children. She seems fine with it, but I—I guess I'm not. I haven't really thought about it before, but somewhere along the way, Nathan has become a surrogate son to me.

My peripheral vision begins to shrink, and I beg God not to let me get a migraine.

The janitor passes without seeing us, and I start breathing again.

You okay? I ask.

He nods.

Come on, I say. We don't have long. The meeting'll be over soon.

We lift the body and are about to step out of the alcove, when the hall lights come on. The lights are bright and it takes a moment for our eyes to adjust.

Whatta we do? Nathan asks.

I check the storage room door across from the classroom and find that it is unlocked.

Here, I say, nodding toward the small closet. Let's stick her in here 'til everyone leaves.

We stand the body upright, leaning it against an assortment of mops and brooms, and close the door.

Let's go see what's going on.

We step out of the alcove and slowly begin to walk back down the hallway. We've only taken a few steps when I see the School Resource Officer, Relentless Rhonda as she's known, walking toward us. My heart sinks and my stomach lurches at the sight of her, but recovers when she nods and smiles.

Relentless Rhonda is a middle-aged white woman with a square, masculine build. She's wearing a green deputy uniform, and walks with just a hint of cop swagger.

Seeming to live here, Rhonda is on the case even when there are no activities and the campus is empty, but when there's a meeting going on like tonight, she'll be the first one here and the last one to leave.

She stops when she reaches us.

What're you two doing up here? she asks. I was just about to lock up.

I hesitate before responding, searching for a good excuse.

Everything okay, Mr. Thomas?

Sure. I say. Why? And call me Randy.

Have you been drinking?

So it's like that. Why is she acting this way? She can't know anything, can she?

Earlier tonight, I say. Just a little.

What are you doing now?

Come on, I tell myself. You're an actor. You can do this. Relax. Tension is your enemy. All the world's a stage. Be the part.

Giving Nate here a ride home, I say, more relaxed, finding my rhythm. We're headed to my car. I parked over by the theater lab.

Isn't it the other way?

You know it is, I say.

She waits, but I don't elaborate.

Well?

He forgot to get something out of his locker, so we've got to go back.

She looks over at Nathan. That true?

Yes, ma'am.

She then studies us for a long moment.

We are both nervous and it shows. I can hear it in our breathing and see it in our sweating faces and shifting eyes. So much for relaxing and being the part.

Okay, she says. But hurry. I'm about to lock all the doors.

I have a key, but don't mention it.

She begins to walk away and we do, too.

We've only walked about ten feet, when Nathan stops.

What is it? I ask.

Hold on a second, he says. I'll be right back.

He then runs back and catches up with Rhonda.

I stand there, more than a little puzzled as I watch Nathan talking softly, even intimately to Rhonda. After a short while, Rhonda pushes Nathan back behind her, draws her gun, and approaches me.

What the— I say, my voice small, my mouth dry. What the hell're you doing?

Step over here, Mr. Thomas, she says, and keep your hands where I can see them.

What? I ask in shock. Why?

Just do it, she says. Now.

I do as I'm told.

What's in the storage closet back there?

I look back at Nathan, but he's looking down.

Nothing, I say. Some cleaning supplies maybe. I don't know.

Open it for me.

What? Why? I ask.

She looks over at the closet.

Rhonda, why're you pointing a gun at me?

Open the door, she says.

Not until you tell me—

She begins to lift her gun, but I still don't move.

Step over here with me, she says, moving toward the closet door.

As I move with her toward the door and what lies behind it, I glance back at Nathan again, but he still refuses to look at me.

As Rhonda approaches the closet, I turn away slightly, reaching into my pocket for my cell phone.

Be very still, she says. I wouldn't want to shoot you by accident.

When she turns back, I slowly pull out my cell phone.

What the hell you think you're doin'?

Calling my wife, I say.

No, you're not.

Yes, I am, I say. Shoot me if you have to, but I can't think straight and she'll know what to do. Her dad's a lawyer. She's just over in the commons at the meeting. She can be here in thirty seconds.

While I'm still talking, Rhonda opens the closet door to reveal the comically wrapped body.

I punch in Dita's number and wait to be connected.

Who are you really calling? Rhonda asks.

I told you, I say. My wife.

She jerks her head back toward Nathan. He says you killed your wife.

What?

That you're making him help you move her body, she says.

I shake my throbbing head, feeling a migraine coming on.

After several clicks, my cell phone connects to Dita's. A moment later, a cell phone begins to ring from within the wrapped package.

My head pounds as my heart drops.

Rhonda rips open a small piece of the wrapping and withdraws Dita's cell phone. She holds it up for me to see. The display reads: Randy Calling.

My murky mind sobers and everything falls into place. Dita *has* been having an affair—with Nathan, who killed her and set me up.

As she pockets the ringing phone, the body shifts and falls out of the closet onto the floor. As it does, the wrapping rips even more and Dita's lifeless hand slips from the hole, her French manicured nails and wedding ring smeared with blood.

Withdrawing her cuffs, Rhonda spins me around, presses me against the painted cinder block wall, and begins to put them on me.

Randy Thomas, I'm arresting you for the murder of your wife, Dita Thomas, she says. You have the right to remain silent. If you give up that right, anything you say can and will be used against you in a court of law. . . .

Facing the hallway now, I look at Nathan again. This time, he looks back. Our eyes lock a moment. He has taken everything from me. Everything. What can I possibly say? How can I—my mind goes completely numb as a small smile appears on his full lips.

I knew he could act. I just had no idea that all this time we had been in a little dram he had scripted for us. Evidently, Dita was a far better actress than I realized, too. She certainly hid her quiet desperation a hell of a lot better than I did. Why didn't she just tell me? If she had, maybe we wouldn't have both been fucked by the same student.

As Rhonda radios for backup, Nathan steps toward me.

Why'd I kill her? I ask. I forget.

He shrugs. Only you can ever really know that, Randy, he says. My guess is you really didn't mean to. Maybe she was threatening to break it off and you just went off. We all go a little mad sometimes.

I begin to lose my vision as the migraine takes hold, and I can't help wondering if my life of quiet desperation is finally over or if it's really just beginning.

Bait and Switch

Andrew Johnson didn't look like the sort of man who'd want help setting up a MySpace account. He didn't look like the sort of man who'd want one, and it wasn't just that he was too old, but the type of too old he was—typical middle-aged Americana. His three-quarter sleeve FSU baseball shirt was faded, dated, and too small, his pregnant paunch pressing against the thin garnet-colored fabric. His going gray hair, which needed cutting, wasn't just out of style, it lacked any style at all (unless cap head counted). His bushy eyebrows were nearly touching, and his sunbaked face was cracked like the clay of a dried-up riverbed.

When he first stepped into the Java Bar and Book Barn, Kody Layfield knew instantly he wasn't here for books or Internet access, which only left coffee, the toilet, or directions. One quick glance up from his laptop, less than a second and back down again, and he knew. If he cared to spend more time he could probably narrow it down even further. For instance, the man didn't strike him as a gourmet coffee drinker. He was more the Waffle House or 7-Eleven type who took it straight up—black, strong, and in a Styrofoam cup—most likely with a Camel. He also didn't appear to be the type of man who'd ask for directions, especially in a small town like this one.

The man surprised Kody by sitting down at the tiny table across from him, but not enough for him to amend his previous inferences.

You Kid? Johnson asked.

At thirteen, Kody had been christened Kody The Kid Layfield because of his sick skills on the computer. In the intervening six years, it had evolved from Kody The Kid to Kody Kid to The Kid to just plain Kid. With his twentieth birthday looming, he wondered how much longer he could be known as any form of kid.

Kody's fine, he said, closing the screen of the online poker game.

Kody didn't want to stop the game. He had a good hand, and needed to win—for the money as well as a psychological sign his luck was changing—but, even if he won every hand, a little online poker wouldn't come close to covering the juice he owed, let alone his marker. For nearly a year, every team he picked, every boxer, every horse, everything, had defied the odds—all in the wrong way. After several years of the kind of preternatural instincts that had the house calling him a prodigy, The Kid was on tilt, trying to recover from the tailspin hurtling him toward the ground.

Keri, the part-time java wench, approached the table, her unnaturally light auburn hair whipping around as she turned toward Johnson.

What can I get you? she asked.

Johnson looked lost for a moment. Ah, he said, a cup of coffee, I guess.

Just plain coffee?

Keri's shorts were so tiny, so soft and clingy, her cami so small, there was far more of her showing than covered—and what was showing was smooth, deeply tanned skin on a slim but muscular body.

He nodded.

As Keri turned to leave, her hair whipping around again, her colorful tattoo peeked out over the thong strap showing above her shorts.

Johnson had shown no reaction to Keri—a first in Kody's experience. Even straight girls and gay guys reacted to the August-in-Florida hotness that was Keri.

Kody stood up, stepped over to Johnson, and placed two fingers on his carotid artery.

What're you do— Johnson began.

Just checking, Kody said. He then returned to his seat without explaining, though it was obvious Johnson didn't get it.

You're some sort of . . . Johnson nodded and motioned toward the laptop in front of Kody as he trailed off.

Gamer? Hacker? Programmer? What? Kody asked.

Whiz, Johnson said.

Yeah, Kody said. I'm a whiz, thus the name.

I wanna hire you.

How much?

Johnson nodded appreciatively. That's the most important question, he said. Twenty-five hundred up front and another twenty-five when it's done.

Kody's eyes widened slightly, and he couldn't help but smile a little.

What is it needs to be done?

Nothing illegal, Johnson said. Nothing immoral. Just a little embarrassing.

Keri brought Johnson's coffee, her flip-flops smacking loudly on the painted cement floor, and placed it on the table in front of him.

When she left, Johnson looked around the shop a little before he started talking again.

The Java Bar and Book Barn was a small storefront on Main Street in downtown Desperation, directly across from Eddie's Bar. The back was a partial kitchen fronted by a counter, atop which sat a couple of napkin-lined wire pastry baskets. The side walls were lined with metal bookshelves, filled mostly with paperbacks and used book club editions. The center space of the building held half a dozen round cafe-style tables and uncomfortable chairs, a stainless steel card holder in the center of each with handwritten reminders that free Wi-Fi Internet access was available.

When Jane and Judy, the lesbian couple from Vermont, had first visited they couldn't believe Desperation had never had a bookstore. After relocating and opening the Java Bar and Book Barn, they knew why. Very few of the souls imprisoned in Desperation were readers, and those who were borrowed books from the library. The few that did actually buy books, and it was very few, bought most of their books at huge discounts from the large chain stores in nearby cities or from online retailers.

I want you to help me set up one of those MySpace things, Johnson said.

That's it?

That's it.

Five G's for something any kid in the country could do wasn't it—not by a long shot, but it was enough money that it didn't matter. Kody needed cash—so much so that he was pretty flexible about how he got it.

When you wanna start? Kody asked.

Right away, Johnson said. The sooner the better.

How about now?

Johnson nodded.

How long you in town for?

How do you know I don't live here?

Small town, Kody said. Know everybody.

I'm here 'til we get this done.

Then you won't be here long.

Johnson shrugged, his expression indicating he didn't care much one way or the other.

Where you from? Kody asked.

Doesn't matter.

They don't have the Internet there?

Johnson smiled and looked around. They got it here, they got it everywhere, he said.

When he reached into his pocket, Kody thought he'd pull out the first half of his money, but he came out instead with a wrinkled photograph and passed it across the table.

Kody took the picture and examined it.

The girl was probably late teens with blonde hair, big brown eyes, a dark, clear complexion, and perfect white teeth in a sexy mouth.

Recognize her?

Kody pursed his lips and tilted his head. She looks vaguely familiar, but she may just have a familiar face. Who is she?

I want you to get me some pictures of girls who look like her, he said. A bunch of them.

There's not a bunch of girls who look like her around here, Kody said.

Not girls, Johnson said. Pictures.

For what?

MySpace, he said.

You want your picture made with girls who look like this?

Not me. Just the girls. Sexy, suggestive photos of the girls.

What kind of MySpace we doin'?

Can you get the pictures?

Kody nodded. I've probably already got a lot that would work, but I'm going to a party on Panama City Beach tonight and I'll get more. It'd help if I knew how you were going to use them.

I just need one girl—like her, Johnson said, nodding toward the picture. Beautiful, carefree, intelligent.

Kody didn't see all that, but didn't say anything.

I want a lot of different girls to choose from, Johnson continued.

What Kody *did* see as his gaze lingered on the picture was a slight resemblance between Johnson and the girl in the photograph. Had he always wanted to be a woman? Was he setting up an online persona of his feminine side?

Will this be your site that includes pictures of a girl or her site? Kody asked, as he returned the picture.

Hers, so we need a girl who doesn't already have a MySpace.

That won't be easy, Kody said. Hell, the whole wide world has a MySpace.

Can you do it or not?

Kody nodded.

Use a wig or something, Johnson said. Shoot them so you can't see much of their faces. I want people who know them to have a hard time recognizing them.

Sure. Okay.

Johnson put the picture away and came out with a roll of one hundred dollar bills. Counting out twenty-five of them, he laid them on the table beside Kody's laptop.

Kody reached for them, but Johnson covered them with his large hand.

Two rules, Johnson said.

Okay.

No more questions.

Kody didn't think he had asked much of anything yet, but nodded.

And once we start, we don't stop until it's done.

Did you find a girl? Johnson asked.

The question came without preamble. He just entered the Java Bar, walked up to where Kody was sitting, and blurted it out.

Creepy bastard, ain't he? Kody thought, but he was glad to see him. Across the street in front of Eddie's, muscle from his shylock was watching him and he didn't want to be alone. Of course, it wasn't just Johnson's company, but his money Kody wanted.

I got lots of girls, Kody said. Pull up a chair and I'll show you.

Johnson drug a chair over beside Kody's and dropped into it.

I put everything I've got online, Kody said, so if you see one you want to use all I have to do is load it onto MySpace.

Kody clicked a few buttons and his screen filled with thumbnails of blonde-haired brown-eyed girls.

MySpace doesn't allow nudity, Kody explained, but I've got some as close as you can get—naked except they've got their hands covering their pink parts.

Johnson studied the pictures and shook his head. More subtle.

Kody brought up another page of pictures.

Her, Johnson said immediately.

Kody clicked on the most girl-next-door chick he had snapped. Her face filled the screen. Even in the snapshot, which was a little out of focus and only showed part of her, you could see a certain insecurity in her downcast brown eyes.

Let me see all the ones you have of her.

Kody opened an entire folder of the girl.

Use her, Johnson said. She well known around here?

Actually, she's visiting from Alabama, Kody said. Staying with her cousin for the summer, and she's so quiet and shy not many people're gonna know her by the time summer's over.

Does she have a MySpace?

Kody shook his head. Amazingly, no.

What's her name?

I'm not sure I should tell you, Kody said. She didn't agree to this or anything, and I thought you just—

It's okay, Johnson said. Doesn't matter. Make the page.

Kody brought up MySpace. We need a username and password, he said. Whatta you wanna call her?

I like April.

Okay, Kody said. How about April Showers?

Johnson nodded.

April Showers may get deflowered, Kody said.

Johnson didn't say anything, and Kody continue to work, clicking through pages and typing in information.

I'm setting up an e-mail account for you at Yahoo so you can get notices when someone posts a comment on your MySpace, he said. We need to create a profile, interests, blurbs, details. Do you want her to have a blog?

A what?

Like a diary everybody can read.

Yeah, Johnson said.

You wanna give me the info or you want me to make it up?

Johnson reached into his pocket and brought out a wrinkled, slightly sweaty sheet of notebook paper and handed it to Kody. Use this.

Kody read the handwritten scrawl of details about April Showers, a cold sweat breaking out on his skin as nausea filled his stomach.

What're we doing this for? Kody asked. I mean, this is really—

No questions, Johnson said. Finish up.

When Kody had finished, Johnson read over it.

April Showers
Female
19 years old

Desperation,
Florida
United States

April's Blurbs
About me:
So here's the deal: I'm a good girl. Not goody-goody, but good. I'm sweet and sensitive, loyal to my friends, kind to animals, mostly play by the rules. I've always been a good girl, but lately I've got another side. Not bad, exactly, but definitely curious about what I've been missing. I don't know. Why am I telling you all this? Who else am I gonna tell? Hope you understand. Maybe you can help me, though I'll probably have to figure it out for myself.

April's Interests
General: The beach, long baths, cold nights and warm sheets, fuzzy navels, tattoos (though I only have 1 so far), hanging out, shopping, eating. I love to eat. Especially sweets.
Music: Love Songs (I know it's sappy, but what can I say?).
Movies: Love Actually, 50 First Dates, Pride and Prejudice, The Notebook.
Television: Grey's Anatomy, The OC, Veronica Mars, Charmed, Buffy (Buffy's still like the best TV show ever).
Books: Not a big reader. I like magazines.
Heroes: I'm still looking.

April's Details
Status: Single, searching (are you out there?)
Here for: dating, fun, to meet Mr. Right
Hometown: Desperation, Florida

Zodiac Sign: Aquarius
Religion: Catholic (mostly lapsed)
Smoke/Drink: No/Yes
Children: Someday
Education: One year of community college.

20 Questions
1. Have you ever been searched by the cops?
Yeah, but no one knows. Not even my closet friends. And only once.

2. Do you close your eyes on roller coasters?
No.

3. Would you rather sleep with someone else, or alone?
I hate sleeping alone.

4. Do you consider yourself creative?
Absolutely.

5. Jennifer Aniston or Angelina Jolie?
Aniston to hang with (I think she'd be the better friend). Jolie to try other things with (told you, I'm curious).

6. Do you know how to play poker?
Only about three people know this, but I've played strip poker before.

7. Have you ever been awake for 48 hours straight?
Only once, but it wasn't as hard as I thought it'd be.

8. Have you ever cheated on a test?
I'm ashamed to say I have, but only once.

9. If you're driving in the middle of the night and no one is around would you run a red light?
Depends on the reason. Can you think of a good one?

10. Do you have a secret that no one knows but you?
Oh yes. A big one.

11. How often do you remember your dreams?
Nearly always if they're sexual, which is most nights. I'm very frustrated right now.

12. What's the one thing on your mind?
Finding that special someone and giving him myself body and soul.

13. Do you believe in love at first sight?
Absolutely!

14. Do you always wear your seatbelt?
Most of the time, but not always.

15. Have you ever narrowly avoided a fatal accident?
Recently, in fact, and it's given me a whole new outlook on life and not wasting a single moment.

16. What do you wear to sleep?
Not a single thing.

17. Left or right?
Left leaning. Right-handed.

18. Does size matter?
Of course.

19. Do you know anyone in jail?
Actually, I do. Long story. Ask me sometime.

20. Do you have a major crush on someone?
You. It's always been you.

Is it what you wanted? Kody asked.

Johnson nodded. Guys can search by area?

Kody nodded. Just put in their zip code and it can bring up all the people within however many miles they specify of their location.

Good.

Now what?

Do a search of a fifty-mile radius and invite everyone in it to be April's friends, and accept anyone who wants to be her friend.

Do you want me to respond to messages as her?

Johnson shook his head. Print them out for me. I'll read them and tell you what to say.

How long we gonna do this?

Not long, he said. It won't take long.

What won't?

Anybody asking to meet her yet?

Nearly a week had come and gone, during which Kody, pretending to be April, had amassed a few hundred friends and messaged back and forth with several of them.

Kody nodded.

The two men were seated across from one another in the Java Bar and Book Barn at the same table at the same time as every other day this week.

Let's hear it.

One guy wants her to come to Club La Vela on Panama

City Beach, Kody said. A couple of them want to take her out.

Where're they from?

One's from Apalach, the other two, Tallahassee.

Who else?

She got two party invitations, he said. One's on Mexico Beach, the other at The Bend, a popular spot on the Apalachicola River.

That's the one, Johnson said. Who is it?

Calls himself Clearwater Casanova.

Arrange a meeting.

At the party?

During, but not at it, he said. Can you do that?

I'm on it, Kody said. He's online right now, so maybe we'll get a quick response.

Good.

Johnson waited as Kody's fingers tapped across the keys.

As he typed, Kody thought about his money problems. He remembered his mom used to say that if you had problems money could fix, you didn't have real problems. If she only knew. The people he owed money to were real problems—so were the crowbars they were going to use to take his life apart.

You know, back when we started all this, five thousand dollars sounded like a lot of money, Kody said.

This works out, you'll get a bonus, he said.

What is it that you're wanting to happen exactly?

Ignoring the question, Johnson asked one of his own. Has he responded yet?

Kody shook his head, his eyes on the screen, his hands still moving over the keyboard.

The two men were quiet a moment.

Can I get the other half of my money today? Kody asked. I'll still do what I'm doing and you can give me a bonus at the end if you want, but I'm in serious need of some coin.

Tell you what, Johnson said. You get ol' Clearwater to meet us alone tonight, and I'll happily hand it over.

The word *we* was not lost on Kody, but he only nodded and continued what he was doing.

Do you know The Bend well? Johnson asked.

Well enough.

Pick a good secluded spot for us to meet, he said. Easy to get to, but hidden and far enough away from the party to be private.

Kody clicked and typed and tapped for a while longer, then said, Done.

Now there's just one more thing I need you to do, Johnson said, and if you will, I'll double what I'm paying you.

What, Kody wondered, could be worth ten thousand dollars?

Beneath a full moon that shimmered on the dark waters of the Apalachicola River and dappled the damp ground with the shadows of jagged cypress tree branches, Kody stood in the small clearing shivering slightly.

Less than five hundred yards away, around a giant bonfire, underage drinking and all the poor judgement that went along with it was taking place.

He had thought this—being here alone, dressed the way he was—was easily worth ten grand, but the longer he had to stand out here in the dark and think about it, the more he wasn't so sure. If anyone saw him or ever found out, he'd never live it down, and he'd certainly have to move—a small Southern town was the last place you could live if a thing like this got out.

The things we do for money, he thought. But it's a lot of money, and he was desperate for it. It wasn't enough to pay off his online gambling debts, but might buy him enough time for his luck to change—and maybe just save his life.

Bait and Switch

Not nearly as clueless as he had pretended to be, Andrew Johnson knew this about Kody, knew he couldn't turn down the opportunity to extend his life a little.

Kody looked around the small clearing again. He was still alone. So far, Clearwater Casanova was a no-show. Beyond the clearing, somewhere in the dense woods and darkness, Andrew Johnson was watching, waiting.

After a while longer, Kody decided it was time to put an end to this exercise in humiliation and began to leave the clearing to search for Johnson.

And that's when it happened.

Tackled from behind, Kody crashed to the ground so hard the small sleeveless summer dress he was wearing ballooned up around his waist and his blonde wig flew off, landing in the dew-damp dirt a few feet away.

He tried to move, shuffle away, but the weight of the guy on top of him and the punch in the face that dazed him prevented it.

He was pretty sure his nose was broken.

When the pale, dark-haired kid in his early twenties on top of him saw that Kody was, in fact, a guy, he came unhinged.

What the fuck? he said, his deep-set, dark-circled eyes growing wide in surprise. Who the fuck're you? You some sort of sick cock-sucking faggot?

The hammer of a revolver being thumbed back shut the kid up, and he raised his hands as the small barrel was pressed against his temple.

That's April Showers, Johnson said. You don't recognize her?

Hey, man, what the fuck's goin' on? he asked. What is this?

This, Johnson said, is the end of the line for you. Your final moments.

Wait a minute now, he began, but Johnson hit him in the head with the butt of the gun.

The blow was so hard it made a cracking sound and knocked him off of Kody.

Kody crawled a few feet away, grabbing his nose with his hands.

Tilt your head up, Johnson said to him. It'll help stop the bleeding.

What are you doing? Kody asked.

Punching this little murderin' prick's ticket.

What? the guy in black asked. You've got the wrong guy. I've never killed anyone in my life. Not even close.

A while back, you began talking to a girl on MySpace, Johnson said. Her name was Sandy Johnson. She was young and innocent, but curious in the way sheltered girls from good homes sometimes are. You two chatted for a while, then you invited her out here to a party, got her to meet you over here in private, away from the group, like separating the weak one from the herd, and you raped her. Not just once. And not just vaginally.

I gave her what she wanted, he said. It's the reason she came out here, the reason she started talking to me online to begin with. She wanted it, to see what it was like hard and rough. She never once said 'no', and I didn't kill her.

The hell you didn't, you twisted little bastard.

You think the cops would let us still be partying out here if some bitch was found dead?

She didn't die here, Johnson said. It was much slower, much more drawn out and painful. You killed her all right; it just took a while for her to die. She stopped talking, quit eating. You can't imagine the hell you consigned her to, you rapist motherfucker.

I—

You don't get to explain, Johnson said. You don't get time to pray, to beg for mercy, to ask for forgiveness. Nothing. You just die.

He then stepped over to him and shot him in the head.

The small pistol made a little pop, and he fell to the ground dead, a tiny trickle of blood snaking down his forehead, over his nose, and across his cheek.

Kody began to cry.

I'm sorry, Johnson said to him.

Was she your daughter?

Johnson shook his head.

Niece?

He shook his head again.

What then?

No relation, he said. Funny, isn't it? Just a coincidence, one of life's little oddities.

I don't understand.

I'm a pro, Johnson said. Hired by the girl's uncle who happens to be in the life. I think you know him. A shylock named Charlie Cash.

Oh, no, Kody said. Oh, God, no. That's why you hired me.

With the vig compounding daily, Kody owed Charlie Cash more than he'd ever be able to win. He was now worth more as an example to other fish than an open account.

Johnson nodded. A retarded kid could set up a MySpace.

Kody began to cry harder.

Like I said, I'm sorry, Johnson said, but you can't fuck with a man like Cash. You can't rape his niece, and you can't fail to pay him what you owe him.

No, please God, no, Kody said. I'll pay him. I swear. I've got ten grand to put toward what I owe him.

Ten Gs of his own money, Johnson said, wiping the gun off with his shirt.

Please, Kody said. I'll do anything.

It's way too late for that, Johnson said, stepping toward him.

I don't want to die, Kody thought. Not yet. Not now.

It's too soon. I've got so much . . . there's too many things I haven't done. My life hasn't even gotten started good yet. I . . . I'm . . . I've got—think, Kody! Think. Figure something—

With his powerful hands, Johnson placed the gun in Kody's hand, forcing his fingers into place. He then squeezed Kody's finger onto the trigger and fired a round in the dead rapist's direction.

Kody tried to pray, tried to think of something to say, something to offer the death dealer in front of him, but nothing would come.

Snake eyes.

Busted.

The loser he had backed was himself.

The house always wins.

I'm truly sorry for how this is going to look, Johnson said. You in a dress. A gay lover's quarrel, homicide/suicide, but . . . he then forced Kody to place the gun to his ear and pull the trigger.

Trapped

When David Martin left Desperation to attend Bible college in Orlando, everyone assumed he'd return for Heather Cox—including David and Heather. Not because they were a couple—they had not been high school sweethearts. Heather was three years younger, the daughter of strict religious parents, and unable to date. But David had chosen Heather, picked her out to be his bride back when they were children, and from that moment, it was just a matter of time.

David filled his days in the usual small town way: football, church, music, cars, and dating—but only casually. Heather was his destiny. Heather spent her time waiting for David, dreaming of the day she would become Mrs. David Martin, falling asleep in his arms every night, waking beside him every morning.

Heather watched as David's athleticism, good looks, and core goodness made him both respected and liked by all. She was so proud when he was voted homecoming king, and couldn't help but think that it was her lobbying efforts among her classmates that had made the difference. And she wasn't even jealous when he and Sandy—the girl everybody knew was just holding her place—became prom king and queen. What did she have to be jealous of? He had picked her. She was his, and everyone knew it.

After David had moved away for college, Heather became a young woman worthy of him, one he could be proud to return for. Heather was one of the most beautiful girls in school, and though she wasn't the most popular and didn't become homecoming and prom queen, or even Miss Desperation High, she was nonetheless a good match for David. And during all this, she saved herself for David, not so much as going on a single date—even attending both her proms alone. David deserved no less. He was going to be the next Billy Graham, only more hip, more popular, better equipped to reach his generation, and he would need a wife devoted to him in the way he was devoted to God. Besides, she was certain he was doing no less for her.

David's return visits home became less and less frequent over the years, which surprised her—particularly when she had come of dating age, but she was sure he was just busy with work (her mom had overheard his mom bragging about how he had been assigned a ministry to the homeless near Church Street Station) and school. Obviously, he had his head down, focused on finishing his degree so he could marry her, and they could get on with their lives together.

When she graduated from high school, she thought for sure she'd hear from him, but then she realized that he had one more year of college. He'd probably wait until he had his degree and a job to come back for her. At first, she wasn't quite sure what to do, then she decided to attend community college and study nursing, working part-time at Peterson's Pharmacy and soon becoming involved in a street ministry of her own.

As her first semester came to a close and Christmas approached, she couldn't help but hope that this Christmas he'd come home bearing an engagement ring. Actually, it was more than hope. Though she would never verbalize it to anyone, she had a knowing. Something deep inside told her David would come home for Christmas with her engagement ring. And she was right. He did—just on another girl's finger.

News of David's engagement spread through Desperation so fast Heather heard about it before she even knew he was in town. She had dashed into the Downtown Deli to pick up a sandwich after leaving the drugstore and before heading to the Christmas tree lot where she volunteered, and the conversation abruptly stopped when she walked in.

In the absence of their words, a pop remake of Jingle Bells could be heard coming through the small speakers mounted in the top corners of the room.

You make a girl nervous when you do that, Heather said, smiling.

There were only three ladies in the small sandwich shop—Moon, the old hippie who owned the place, Big Wanda, a retired school teacher and the biggest gossip in town, and Mayor Mary Alice, who wasn't as malicious as Big Wanda, but always seemed to be around when dirt was being dished.

Sorry, dear, Moon said, her pale round face pained, but we just heard.

We're so sorry, little darling, Big Wanda said. We all thought the two of you would wind up together.

What're you talking about? Heather asked.

Big Wanda tried to suppress the wicked smile lifting her fat jowls, but not very hard. You haven't heard?

Heard what?

About David, dear, Mary Alice said, losing Heather's vote in the next election—the first one in which she'd be eligible to cast a ballot.

What about David? she asked, her frustration unmasked.

He came home engaged to some big city girl, Big Wanda said.

She had thought of it as a mild winter until tonight, but now she couldn't stop shivering. The wind blowing off the bay into the vacant lot where she and the other volunteers sold Christmas trees was damp and icy, and her small North Florida coat was inadequate.

She wanted to go home. No, that wasn't exactly right. She just didn't want to be here. Every other night she had been the first to arrive and the last to leave, gladly taking double shifts so that the other volunteers could attend Christmas parties and go caroling. With her sweet, cheerful disposition, which still stood out even during this season when most everyone was wishing joy to the world, she had moved more trees than anyone. It was for a good cause—the proceeds were going toward opening the Samaritan Center, an outreach for the poverty-stricken of Desperation—and she loved to see how happy the full, fresh trees made the families who purchased them. But no more. Not tonight. She had to go. They'd have to understand.

She had made her excuses and was just about to depart when David's family strolled beneath the row of lights strung across the entrance and down the center aisle. Cheryl, David's mom, who had never thought Heather was good enough for her son, was leading the way, walking arm-in-arm with the girl who was living Heather's life. David and his dad, the man everyone in town called Big Dave, were several paces behind.

Remembering that the Martins had already bought a tree two weeks ago, Heather realized what was happening the moment before it did. Cheryl had brought David's fianceé by to show her off. She had won, and this was a victory lap. And she wasn't even subtle about it. She walked right up to Heather, a gloating grin on her wind-reddened face.

Heather, have you met David's wife, Stephanie? Cheryl asked.

Heather was unable to speak. Wife? Were they really already married?

Heather could tell Stephanie was sizing her up, Stephanie's cool blue eyes deciding she was superior. She was beautiful, Heather had to admit, but she was all wrong for David.

Turning to the two men trailing them, Cheryl said, *David, you remember little Heather, don't you?*

In one catty question, she had not only dismissed Heather, but denied her relationship with her son.

From the look of sick surprise, the flash of pity in his eyes, Heather could tell David was as much a victim of this little ambush as she was. Thank God for that.

Ma-um, David said, which was about as much frustration as he ever showed to her. *Of course, I remember the prettiest, sweetest girl in town. How are you?*

Heather attempted a smile and nodded, still unable to find her voice.

Stepping between his mom and Stephanie, David leaned in and gave Heather a hug.

It was meant as a quick, casual gesture, but it grew intense, Heather clinging to him, pressing her body into his, feeling his warmth and strength, knowing she needed much, much more of them than this brief exchange could offer her.

Let go now, dear, Cheryl said to Heather, as if she were the only one holding on. *He's a married man.* Then turning to Stephanie added, *I think the poor little thing's always had a bit of a crush on our boy.*

While Cheryl was talking and Stephanie was laughing, David whispered in Heather's ear, Meet me at the pier in an hour.

The Christmas lights and decorations on lampposts and in store windows made downtown Desperation seem peaceful and magical. The streets were mostly empty, all the shops closed, only a handful of pedestrians spread around the sidewalks and the occasional car passing by.

As Heather walked toward the pier, she wondered why David wanted to meet with her in private, what he had to say. What *was* there to say?

Her tear-streaked cheeks were cold and numb, an outward manifestation of an inward and spiritual condition.

How had this happened? David's calling was too important to be—then she realized what was going on. This was an attack of hell itself. Satan was attempting to destroy David's ministry before it got started good. If *she* knew what David was destined for—to be the next Billy Graham—then surely the Devil did.

Stephanie was a pawn of the dark side. She was too stuck-up to serve others, too self-centered to share David with the world that so desperately needed him. Did David see it? Did he know what was going on? Was that why he wanted to meet with her?

When she reached the dark gazebo at the end of the short pier, David was waiting for her.

Thanks for coming, he said.

Sure, she said.

Enveloped in darkness, the black waters of the bay slapping at the pilings beneath them, the lights of Desperation in the distance, they were alone and hidden.

I had to see you, he said. To apologize. To explain.

The paper mill was hidden behind an outcropping of land that jutted into the bay and the tall pines it held, but its lights shimmered on the surface of the water, its steel structures reflected as in dark shards of glass.

I'm so sorry, he said. I've sinned, not just against God, but against you.

They were close, but not touching, and she was glad she couldn't really see his face and he couldn't see hers.

I don't have any excuses, he said. I was tempted, led astray by my own lust. I'm far weaker than I thought I was, not fit for the ministry.

Don't say that, she said. You're—

I just wanted you to know that I did intend on coming back for you, he said. Mom wouldn't have stopped me. No one would have.

Except Stephanie.

I didn't want anything serious with her, he said. I really didn't. I just . . . things happened and . . . I'm sorry.

Why'd you marry her?

I had to, he said. I couldn't just . . . and not.

He's such a good man, she thought. He couldn't sleep with her and not marry her. God, where were you? Why didn't you protect your servant from the evil temptress?

You slept with her?

I'm so sorry, he said. I don't even remember it. We were at a party, and I guess the punch was spiked. The whole night's a blur.

You just took her word for it? she asked. You probably just passed out. Don't you see what—

She's pregnant, he said. It's like the sin of King David. I got her pregnant.

For a long moment, she couldn't speak.

I'm so, so sorry, he said. I don't want to be married to her, but it's my fault. I'm reaping what I sowed.

How do you even know the baby's yours? she asked.

He started to say something, but stopped.

David, she said. It's probably not even yours.

She's not like that, he said. She wouldn't do that.

But he didn't sound like he believed what he was saying.

I've got to go, he said. I just wanted you to know how sorry I was, and how I wish things could be different.

They can be, she said. *We* can be.

No, he said. I can't divorce her. You know that. God hates divorce.

But your calling, she said. Your ministry. You've got to—

I'm not the man you think I am, he said. I'm not just weak. I'm evil. I have bad thoughts all the time now. Hate in my heart. Bitterness and unforgiveness.

David, I know you, she said. You're a—

You have no idea how wicked I am, he said. No idea.

You're human, sure, but you're not wicked, she said. Don't say that.

I just feel like I'm going to suffocate, he said. I feel like I can't move, can't breathe. I just want out. He hesitated, but she could tell he had more to say, so she waited. Sometimes I just wish she'd have an accident or something. Just wreck her car or slip in the shower. I know how awful that sounds—I told you I'm wicked—but I just can't help it.

He still loved her. She should have never doubted that.

Dear God, he was a good man. So faithful, so trusting, so honorable. No wonder God had chosen him. No wonder Satan was trying so hard to destroy him. But that was not something she was going to let happen.

She went straight home and dug out her Bible from beneath a stack of books on her night stand, a pang of guilt pricking her conscience for how long it had remained untouched, unread. She had never been the Bible student David was, and the longer he had stayed away the less of one she had become. But she did recall that the story of King David and his great sin was somewhere in one of the books of Samuel, and it didn't take her long to find it.

As she read, she thought about what her David had said. He was a lot like Israel's greatest king—a man after God's own heart, who had passion and purity and a mission, and was in a difficult position. She was looking for guidance, wondering what David's message had been, praying for the wisdom to know what to do and the strength to do it.

What had David been trying to tell her? It was no accident he had likened his sin to that of King David. In his mind, he had done what the king had done—trapped himself by impregnating a woman. She had serious doubts that her David had actually done that—he was in a trap of another kind—but he believed he had. King David had an adulterous affair with Bathsheba, the wife of Uriah, and had Uriah killed.

There was a footnote in her Bible that said the reason God forgave David for what he had done was because he repented. It referenced Psalm 51, which she turned to and read. And read and read again, committing to memory the poetic cry for mercy.

When she finished reading and closed her Bible, returning it to the top of the stack this time, Heather wondered if David had compared his sin to King David's because he felt like what he had done was actually adultery because in his heart he was married to her. She also wondered if he was planning to kill Stephanie or was asking her to.

The more she thought about it, the more Heather knew for certain David would never ask her to kill anyone—not even the Satanic Stephanie—but she couldn't let him do it. She had to protect him, keep his hands clean. She knew from her reading that God had not let King David build the temple because he had blood on his hands. Her David had to fulfill his mission. She had to make sure of it, but how?

King David had sent Uriah into battle on the front line. What could she do? She wasn't seriously considering killing someone, was she? She couldn't do that. Not even for David. Or could she? She had always believed she could do anything for him, but murder? King David had done it, but even he had not used his own hands. Using the arrow of an enemy archer is very different than killing someone yourself.

God, this so difficult. Why couldn't the evil bitch just have an accident? It'd make everything so much easier. She was thinking this, stocking the shelves of the feminine hygiene section, when the evil bitch strolled into Peterson's.

You must be Stephanie, Kelby Peterson, the wife of the pharmacist said.

Heather was a little over halfway down the center aisle, kneeling, hidden. She could hear what was taking place, but couldn't see it. Except for Carl Peterson, the pharmacist, who was behind his counter, the store was empty.

I seem to have come up here to your little town without my shampoo, Stephanie said. And I simply can't use my husband's Head & Shoulders. Do you have Deep Shine sea kelp crème by Rusk?

She knows good and well a small town drugstore like this one doesn't have anything like that, Heather thought. She's just being condescending.

Sea kelp, no ma'am, Kelby said.

After a long sigh of frustration, Stephanie asked, Well, what is the best shampoo and conditioner you have?

Ah, well, I'm not exactly sure, Kelby said. They're right over here.

The two women walked down to the center of the first aisle, Heather no longer even pretending to be doing anything but attempting to overhear their conversation.

Is this it? Stephanie asked.

All four shelves, yes, ma'am.

I've never even heard of any of these, she said. Which of them's the most expensive?

This set here, Kelby said. This leave-in conditioner really works wonders.

Fine, she said. Do the Martins have an account here?

Ah, yes, but—

Charge them to their account, she said. And I need some KY, too.

The thought of David being intimate with this vile woman infuriated Heather, and she could feel waves of heat emanating from her flushed face.

I need the biggest tube you have, Stephanie was saying as the two women approached her aisle.

Ah, sure, Kelby said. Okay.

When they reached the center aisle, Heather was hard at work shelving boxes of condoms.

Stephanie stopped when she saw Heather.

Well, if it isn't my David's first little crush, she said.

He's my David, and everyone knows it, Heather thought, as she continued working, refusing to engage.

Here's the, ah . . . Kelby said, motioning to what to her were unmentionables.

Give me two of those large tubes, she said. Our David's downright insatiable.

How can she talk about him like that? What's wrong with her? It wasn't just that she didn't deserve David. She didn't deserve to live.

She knew what she had to do.

She had to protect David. No matter the cost.

Giving herself over to the dark thoughts beginning to permeate her mind, she tried to recall what she had learned from her nursing classes that might help her. She'd like for it to look like an accident or at least not point to her. Though she was willing to lay down her life for David, she'd rather them be able to spend the rest of their lives together, praying to God, as King David had, to have mercy on them according to his unfailing love, and putting this whole bad dream behind them.

It took her a while, but following thorough research, Heather decided on a botanically derived poison—something that acts fast, has a high toxicity, is easy to find, and can be absorbed through the skin. She chose nicotine, the oldest insecticide still in use. All she had to do was steep some cigarette tobacco in water for twenty to thirty minutes, then simmer it until it was concentrated into a syrup-like substance.

Heather knew the nicotine would constrict Stephanie's arteries, including those that supplied blood to her heart, but she tried not to think about it. When they had constricted the blood supply to her heart, the muscle would be diminished and she'd suffer a heart attack or a lethal cardiac arrhythmia. Of course an ME would have no problem detecting a high level of nicotine in Stephanie's blood, urine, and tissue. If he looked for it. But he probably wouldn't, and even if he did, there would be no way to trace it back to her. From her reading,

Heather knew that most routine toxicological screens tested for alcohol, sedatives, narcotics, amphetamines, marijuana, cocaine, and aspirin. If the poison used was not in one of these classes, and hers was not, it could easily be missed. The small town doc who served as ME would most likely attribute the death to a heart attack or cardiac arrhythmia, and David would be hers again.

On Sunday morning, while David was in the pulpit of Desperation First Baptist, and his parents and new wife were gazing up reverently from the pews, Heather crept into the Martin residence like a thief in the night with her little bottle of nicotine.

Several times, as she made her way through the heavily decorated home, she hesitated, actually beginning to leave a time or two, but she prayed for strength, for fortitude to finish the task she had been given.

Eventually, she realized that the only way she could get through this was to stop thinking about what she was doing and just do it—to focus on her actions and not think about their consequences.

In the moist shower stall of David's bathroom, next to his Head & Shoulders, were the two bottles Stephanie had charged at the drugstore. With trembling gloved hands, she removed the cap of the leave-in conditioner, carefully poured in the nicotine, replaced the cap, and returned the bottle to the small damp ledge.

It was just that simple. By using the conditioner to administer the poison, she had ensured it would have time to be absorbed through her scalp and into her bloodstream.

Stephanie was dead the next day.

At the memorial service, Heather read Psalm 51, which surprised most people. It wasn't a passage often read at funerals.

Have mercy on me, O God, according to your unfailing love, according to your great compassion blot out my transgressions, she read—actually recited—with such conviction that the words seemed her own. Wash away all my iniquity and cleanse me from my sin. For I know my transgression, and my sin is always before me. Cleanse me with hyssop and I will be clean; wash me, and I will be whiter than snow. Create in me a pure heart, O, God, and renew a right spirit in me. Don't cast me from your presence or take your Holy Spirit from me.

The power of her performance, if that's what it could be called, was aided by the slight quiver in her voice and the occasional tear rolling down her cheek. It was just the right balance of sadness and sincerity. No hysterics, no theatrics. Just genuine grief.

The surprising scripture selection was the least of the surprises that day, though, and soon forgotten by most of those in attendance. The funeral, or more precisely the reason for it, was so astounding that it overshadowed everything else, and left most everyone in shock.

First Stephanie, and then the next day, David—and both in the shower. Foul play was suspected, but everything had been ruled out except for poisoning, and it would still be a while before toxicology tests would be back.

As Heather concluded her reading at David's memorial service and was helped back to her seat, her knees buckling several times, the entire congregation seemed to be thinking the same thing, David and Stephanie had been so young, so active, so healthy. How could it have happened? Some theorized that the lovely Stephanie had simply slipped in the shower, but that poor David had died of grief. Life and death are mysteries, the preacher had said, but we can take comfort in knowing that everything is in God's control.

Most puzzling of all, however, was the fact that the day after David's memorial service, Heather Cox had been found dead in David's shower, apparently in the same manner David and his wife had died. Only this time, the cause of death appeared to be self-inflicted. Unlike Stephanie and David, Heather had left a note.

She had come into the Martin house like so many others from the church, bearing food, and while others had reheated the food or expressed again their condolences, she had crept upstairs to David's room. Lingering for just a moment, she breathed in his smell, the sweet, familiar scent bringing tears to her eyes.

Oh God, what have I done?

The answer was immediate. Something I can't live with.

Withdrawing the note she had previously prepared, she carefully placed it on the floor next to the small fiberglass enclosure-cum-death chamber.

On a single sheet of tear-stained paper, she had written two different psalms. The first was Psalm 51, which she had read at David's memorial service, and the second was Psalm 9, verse 16: The wicked is snared by the work of his own hands.

Janie's Got a Gun

The slurping sounds she's making are loud, and he's scared someone's going to hear. Other girls, the couple there had been, had been so quiet. Of course, no other girl had ever gone down on him in the mechanical closet next to the band room before.

She uses her hand, too. Most girls, well the other two who had made any attempt at all at giving him oral, only used their mouths. But Janie gripped him tight with her long, narrow, French-manicured fingers, using her hand and her mouth, and making him feel it from the tip all the way down the shaft and to his toes.

Janie's got a gun.

The line from the song keeps playing in his head, and it actually adds to the experience.

Before this moment, he didn't know girls like this really existed. He'd heard other guys talk about girls who *couldn't* get enough, who *had* to have it, but always thought that the stuff of rural legend. Making up shit is what people do for fun in Desperation. Hell, nothing else to do—except have your new girlfriend, the prettiest, sweetest girl in school, skip class to pull you into a closet, unzip your Levi's, and take you in her mouth.

God, she's so good. How'd he get so lucky? Popular and attractive enough, he isn't the type of guy who usually gets the Janies of the world. But he's got her now, and he's not letting go—ever.

Janie's got a gun.

I love you so much, he says.

She mumbles something that sounds like, Love you, too.

Does she really love me? She sure acts like she does. But he can't help thinking she wouldn't even be with him if the quarterback was still around. They'd only gotten together after he he had gone, and Teddy lives in fear he'll return. Can he really expect Janie to stay with a skateboarder and musician if she could be with a quarterback and homecoming king?

Her movements intensify, and he knows it's just a matter of moments before he explodes. Does she mean for him to do it in her mouth? He kinda thinks she does.

Oh God, he says, as he feels the beginning of that out-of-control feeling, and a wave as big as the ones in the Gulf during a hurricane well up inside him. Closing his eyes, he sees elongated shapes and colors, as if his mind is a giant lava lamp.

After his explosion, he's too sensitive for her up and down motions, so he lifts her head. She stands and kisses him, something he hadn't intended her to do. Not sure what to do, but too in love to care, he kisses her back. Right now, he can only do what Janie wants, as if she really does have a gun.

When Teddy and Janie step out of the mechanical closet, Mr. Thompson, the guidance counselor, is standing there.

Mr. Thompson, Teddy begins, we were just looking for—

I know what you're looking for, and it looks to me like you found it. Teddy, you come with me. Janie go back to class, and I'll call you up later.

As they walk through the school toward Mr. Thompson's office, Teddy thinks about what might happen to him, what he'd say or do. Mr. Thompson's cool. If someone had to catch them, he's glad it's him. He won't make a bigger deal of it than it is. He won't freak out, won't tell their parents or Warden Murray.

More than anything, Teddy's worried about Janie. He can't imagine how embarrassed she must feel, how ashamed she must be. What she had done was so . . . It had made her so vulnerable. He doesn't want this to be a traumatic experience for her, doesn't want her to associate what she had done or any aspect of their relationship with something that is negative or shameful.

Genuinely concerned for her, he's also really hoping that nothing about them getting caught would make her reluctant to do that to him again.

Mr. Thompson's office is the largest in the school, and the most cluttered. His desk is buried beneath student records, printouts, file folders, and papers. The built-in shelves along one wall are littered with tracts, pamphlets, books, and videos from every career imaginable, especially those of the armed services. On the opposite wall is nearly its mirror image, except rather than careers, the virtues and strengths of colleges are extolled. Across the room from his desk, a long wooden conference table surrounded by wooden chairs with cushioned seats is covered with cardboard box after cardboard box of standardized tests.

Have a seat.

Teddy removes a stack of file folders from one of the two chairs in front of Thompson's desk, places them atop the stack already in the other chair, and sits down.

For a moment, Mr. Thompson doesn't say anything, just considers Teddy.

First, you're not in any kind of trouble or anything. I just want to talk to you, help you if I can.

Thanks.

What's wrong with what you did isn't necessarily the act itself—whatever that might be—but the inappropriateness of the time and place. Understand?

Teddy nods.

It's not something we can do at school—as much as we might like to.

As Teddy nods again, he can't keep his lips from forming a little appreciative smile. Mr. Thompson is all right.

Mr. Thompson—Teddy doesn't even know his first name—is a single, late-twenties or early-thirties guy, still thin, attractive, and cool enough for several of the girls and a couple of the female teachers to think he's hot. Teddy can't really tell whether a guy is handsome or not, but he suspects it is Mr. Thompson's genuine kindness and compassion that makes him so appealing.

I *am* worried about Janie, though.

You are?

You're a good guy, Teddy, and I'm glad she's with you. I was surprised when you two started dating. She usually goes for bad boys. It's a good sign that she picked you.

Thanks.

But I think she needs help.

Really?

I'd like to help you help her. Do you love her?

Teddy nods.

I'm putting a lot of trust in you, but I know you can handle it. If I didn't think you could and I didn't believe it absolutely essential to save Janie's life I wouldn't be doing this.

Save her life?

I could get in a lot of trouble.

For what?

Have you noticed anything different about Janie?

Like? Teddy asks, his voice growing defensive.

Does she seem more . . . ah, sexual than other girls? More experienced?

You callin' her a slut?

Of course not, Thompson says. Nothing like that. I'm worried about her. I care for her the way I care for you.

Just tell me.

Answer my question first. Is she more sexual than your other girlfriends?

I guess.

Is sex the focus of your relationship?

Teddy takes a moment to think about it, but he doesn't need to.

I think she's been sexualized from a very early age, the counselor says. I'm almost certain of it.

Sexualized?

It's like having the switch to your sexuality turned on before it's time.

How? By who?

That's what I'd like to figure out. I've tried talking to her about it, but, as you can imagine, she's very reluctant. That's normal. Most victims are. And I don't want to push. I tried to get her to talk to a female counselor, but she wouldn't. If I insist I'm afraid it'll do more harm than good. That's why I think you could help. If you're willing.

I don't know.

I understand. It's a big thing to ask. But if you can't or won't, the only other alternative I have is to turn this over to Department of Children and Families—I should anyway, but then it'll turn into something even more traumatic for her, and if he just denies it and she doesn't cooperate, it'll just make her life worse.

Who's *he*?

I don't know for sure.

Who do you think it is?

Are you in?

Hell yeah. Who is it?

It's just a suspicion, so don't do anything stupid. We've got to be sure. And you've got to be careful. It could be very dangerous. I think he may have killed the last guy she was dating, Dusty. I did some checking because his new school never requested his records. He disappeared right after he moved.

Just tell me who it is.

Her stepdad.

It's an epidemic, really.

What?

Molestation. So many young girls living in a house with a grown man who's not their dad.

Hadn't thought of that.

All I'm asking you to do right now is look for the signs.

The signs?

Of sexual abuse. I don't know if it happened when she was as a child and it stopped, or if it started then and is continuing, or if it started recently. The signs should confirm for us if it has happened or *is* happening.

You think he could be having sex with her now?

Maybe. Don't get too—

What're the signs?

Take it easy. If you're too overwrought, you won't do her any good.

The signs?

Probably won't have them all. Just casually observe. Don't let her know. Common behavioral indicators include depression, eating disorders, sleep disturbances, nightmares, school problems, withdrawal from family and friends and normal activities, excessive bathing or poor hygiene—

How can it be both?

No, it'll be one or the other. Either she'll be compulsively clean, trying to wash him off of her, or she'll try to stay dirty, want to smell in order to repel him.

Teddy nods.

Other signs include anxiety, running away, passive or overly pleasing behavior—

She certainly knows how to please, Teddy thinks.

—low self-esteem, self-destructive behavior, drug or alcohol problems, hostility or aggression, cutting, suicide attempts, and heightened sexual activity or promiscuity.

Hell, that's half the kids I know.

Well, yeah, several studies say one in four girls and one in five boys is sexually abused by the age of eighteen.

No way.

It's hard to believe, I know, but it's true. Seventy-five percent of the abusers are family members.

Teddy shakes his head, thinking about his own parents, how protective they are, how good. I just can't believe—

You come from a good home and can't even imagine it, but it's true.

Teddy has a hard time believing this about Janie—and there are signs, he suspected something even before Mr. Thompson called him into his office—but a quarter of his class? How can that be? He just can't believe that out of Keli,

Hali, Katelin, Terri, Shelby, Robin, Harley, and Brandi, the varsity cheerleaders, that two of them had been molested.

Tell you what, Thompson says, handing him a couple of printouts of Internet pages. Read these, look for the signs, and come back and see me in a couple of days.

That night, unable to eat or sleep or think about anything else, Teddy lies on his bed reading one of the articles Mr. Thompson had given him titled, "Teenage Promiscuity Linked to Sexual Abuse."

There are typically two responses to the experience of sexual abuse: promiscuity and abstinence. In the first group, the reaction to an awakened sexuality leads to a sexualized lifestyle in which the adolescent's experience of abuse leads to his or her own sexual acting out. In the second group, their sexuality is essentially turned off, and they abstain from sex altogether because of unpleasant experiences and painful memories.

Study after study points to the same sad reality: the developmental impact of sexual abuse leads to symptoms of maladjustment and problems of depression, anxiety, and other internalizing disorders, as well as externalizing acting out such as dissociation, conduct disorders, aggressiveness, and inappropriate or early sexual behavior and activity.

Studies also show that there is a direct link between sexual abuse and above-average rates of alcohol abuse, promiscuity, and other risky behaviors. Children and teens often move from being victimized to self-victimization, moving from one area of self-abuse to another—from alcohol to drugs to harder drugs, often using their altered state to act out their promiscuity.

Teddy stops reading. He has to. He can't take any more. Besides, he can no longer ignore the vibrating phone on his bedside table.

Flipping open his phone, he begins to read the numerous texts Janie has sent him.

Give me a T, is all the first one says. Give me an E, the second one. Give me a DD—Y. Whatta you got? Teddy. Now open your window for a real big surprise.

He rolls off his bed and pulls the string to raise his blinds. Standing there in his mom's flowerbed is Janie in her Desperation High cheerleading uniform, complete with pom poms.

Pulling his window open, he whispers, What are you doin'?

Crawling through the window, her blonde hair whipping about, she says, Making your night—maybe your life. Every guy wants to score with a cheerleader, right?

He tries to smile, but can't. All he can think about is what Mr. Thompson had said, what he has read.

As she speaks, he detects the faint scent of alcohol beneath her breath freshener.

The cheerleading uniform appears to have been designed especially to show off Janie's tall, athletic build, her long arms and legs, her little heart-shaped ass.

Tossing her pom poms on the floor, she falls back on the bed, spreads her legs, and pulls up her skirt—underneath which, she wears nothing.

Come on, I'm ready, she says. I had to wait out there so long, I started without you.

As he takes off his shirt and drops it onto the article he had been reading, he thinks about how Janie had quit cheering in the middle of football season, after seeming to live for cheering for several years before that, and wonders if that's one of the signs Mr. Thompson had recruited him to look for—*this* certainly is.

Did I ever tell you that your mom and I wouldn't be together today—and you wouldn't have been born—had she not crawled through my window in college?

Breakfast the next morning, mom and dad at the table.

Teddy shakes his head.

It's true. We were broken up—I thought for good. I was going back home for the summer the next day, and that night she climbed through my window. We got back together and made you.

Teddy raises an eyebrow at his mom.

You're welcome, she says, smiling. But I think you would still be here. Your dad was leaving, but I had the distinct impression he'd be back for me.

His dad nods. Almost certainly, but my point for telling you this is, I know how exciting it can be to have a girl climb in your window.

His dad's right, he thinks. Having a beautiful girl crawl through your bedroom window in a cheerleading uniform, spread out on your bed, and ask you to make love to her, is so exciting it might make you drop trou and slide in bed and inside her, even if doing so might constitute taking advantage of her victimization.

But, his dad adds, if that's the only way she comes and goes, it might be . . . a little . . . I don't know, disrespectful.

He should tell them about what Mr. Thompson suspects, but can't. Not yet. Not until they meet her, see how wonderful she is. Then, he'll enlist their help. It's not that they wouldn't help now. They would. But then their first impression of Janie would always be of a girl being fucked by her stepdad.

We'd like to meet her, his mom says. We promise not to scare her off.

Scare her off? Teddy thinks. If she's like everybody else, she'll want you to adopt her.

Ditching second period, Teddy makes his way to Mr. Thompson's office. He'd been meaning to report back to him for the past few days, but Janie is almost always around—and he really doesn't want to tell him what he's discovered.

Passing through the main office quickly so as not to give the school secretary time to ask for his pass, he winds around the back hallway passing Warden Murray's and the assistant's offices to find the guidance counselor's door closed.

As he raises his hand to tap on it, the door opens and he is face to face with Janie, Mr. Thompson, showing her out, a few feet behind her.

Janie looks surprised and a little alarmed to see him. What're you doin' here? she asks.

Teddy freezes.

I asked him to come by and look at some college programs I want him to consider, Mr. Thompson says.

That's fast, Teddy thinks. She might actually believe it. Good save, Mr. T.

You? Teddy asks.

Turning in my volunteer hours for the Bright Futures Scholarship. You're looking at schools?

Yeah.

I thought you were going to Gulf Coast? Janie asks, wince on her face, betrayal in her voice.

Teddy shrugs. Just looking at all the options.

I thought *we* are going together. You know Brian'll never let me go off to college.

Relax, I'm not gonna leave you.

I don't mean . . . I . . . I'm not trying to hold you back.

It's my fault, Mr. Thompson says. I've been pressuring him. I didn't realize you two had plans together. He's just looking at them because he's a nice guy.

Teddy nods. I'm not going anywhere without you. Come on. I'll walk you back to class.

I've seen the signs, Teddy says.

He's back in Thompson's office after walking Janie to class. Second period is one of only two they don't have together.

You have?

I didn't want to. Tried not to, but they're there.

So you think she's been or is being . . .

Yeah, Teddy says. I don't want to think about it, but . . . yeah.

Thompson nods, seeming to consider Teddy.

Whatta we do?

Have you talked to her?

Teddy shakes his head.

Is it her stepdad?

Teddy shrugs.

You hear her say he'd never let her go off to college?

Teddy nods. And called him Brian.

Try to confirm that's it's him.

And then?

How do you feel about homicide?

Can we hang at your house tonight? Teddy asks.

They are in the lunchroom. Janie's stepdad has once again brought her fresh, hot food from town, and she's sharing it with Teddy.

What's wrong with yours?

You ashamed of me?

What? *No.*

We never hang at your house.

They hadn't been together long, but long enough for it to be weird she didn't invite him to her house.

Brian's funny about my boyfriends. I just don't want to subject you to his scrutiny.

I can handle it.

I know that. But I can't.

Why?

I just can't. Can we leave it at that?

I want to know.

She hesitates.

Has he always brought you lunch?

Not always. Haven't always known him.

How long he been with your mom?

He's not. They split.

And you live with him?

She got a job in Tallahassee. I wanted to finish school here. Aren't you glad?

Why can't you deal with it?

Tallahassee?

Me being around your . . . ah, Brian.

I don't want to talk about it.

I do.

He's very critical.

I can handle it.

So you say.

But you can't?

No.

Why?

'Cause he's so good at it. He can find flaws and exploit them better than anyone I know.

Even in you?

No. I'm the only person he's never criticized.

Never?

Not ever.

He's critical of your mom and not you?

She nods.

So he'll find my flaws—not a hard thing to do—and point them out. So what?

So I don't want to hear it.

'Cause you'll start to believe it?

Always have in the past.

The house is modest, utilitarian, immaculate; the stepdad, muscular, disciplined, conservative. Neither is what Teddy expected.

Welcome to our humble little home, Brian Bosworth says, extending his hand.

Bosworth's shake is firm, but not overly so. There is nothing in it that attempted to establish dominance, no intimidation.

Janie had told him that Bosworth used to be a cop. It fit. And it isn't just his close-cropped hair or rigid manner, but the wariness in his eyes.

It's nice to have you, he continues. It's been a while since Janie's had a young man over.

Thank you, sir. It's nice to be . . . thanks for having me.

Just relax and make yourself at home . . . Bosworth raises his eyebrows and looks as if he is waiting for something.

Teddy.

Teddy. Would you like something to drink, Teddy?

I'm good. Thanks.

Bosworth leads Teddy into the small den. There is still no sign of Janie, and he tries to look for her without being obvious.

The tiny room is sparsely furnished; both the couch and chair, which creaked loudly as they sat, are draped with slipcovers that pull and gather and fold in on you. Teddy sinks into the worn sofa so that Brian, in the chair directly across, looks down on him.

Across the room, in the far back corner, is an enormous gun cabinet, filled with more weapons than Teddy's ever seen anywhere but a gun shop.

Did he bring me in here just so I'd see his arsenal?

For a long, almost unbearable moment, Bosworth looks at Teddy without saying anything.

Where's Janie? Teddy asks.

Finishing dinner. It's almost done. She'll be out in a minute, but she can hear us if you want to say hi.

Hey Janie.

When there is no reply, Bosworth, laughing, shrugs. I thought she could hear us. Sorry.

He's so polite, Teddy thinks. Is that part of his strategy? He trying to get me to lower my guard?

So, what do your parents do? Bosworth asks.

My dad's a correctional officer. My mom sells real estate.

And you?

At first Teddy doesn't say anything. He isn't sure what the man means. I'm a . . . I go to school with Janie. I'm a student.

Oh, I know that. I meant when you're not in school.

Teddy shrugs. See Janie as much as I can. Hang out. Play video games.

Video games?

Teddy nods tentatively.

Do you have a job? Play sports?

No, sir. Not really. I do some odd jobs for my neighbor from time to time.

I see. Well, that's okay.

Is it Teddy's imagination, or is everything he says and does, every word, every expression, every gesture, an insult? He's polite about it, but he's judging Teddy, weighing him, finding him wanting.

And it continues over dinner.

Janie's appearance only heightens the tension, intensifies Bosworth's insults, though they're still veiled in politeness, but that isn't the worst of it. Teddy can take Bosworth's jabs and cuts. It's the way he flirts with Janie that threatens to upset the equilibrium of propriety.

This is your best yet, dear, Bosworth says, holding up a fork full of meatloaf. Is there anything you can't do well?

He treats her more like a wife than a daughter, Teddy thinks, clenching his fists beneath the table.

Though Janie beams appreciatively at his praise, Teddy thinks he sees revulsion beneath her carefully constructed facade.

So, Ted, what do you plan to do after graduation?

College.

Really?

You sound surprised.

Do I? he asks, sounding even more surprised now. Looking over at Janie, he adds, Did I?

Janie shrugs and when Bosworth looks away, she gives Teddy an *I'm sorry* expression.

I don't think I did, Ted, but if I did, it might be that most of the kids around here don't go to college. No offense. It's just a fact. So which school do you plan to attend?

Gulf Coast.

Bosworth winces slightly and purses his lips. You really ought to reconsider that. I mean if you're serious about actually finishing, getting a degree and a good job. Besides, nothing makes a man out of a boy more than going off to college.

He's trying to get rid of me, Teddy thinks, eliminate the competition. Why's that? he asks.

It's easy to blow off community college, drop out, say you'll go back, and never get around to it. I mean, come on, it really is like thirteenth grade. But if you move away to school, get as far away from home as you can, you're more committed, much more likely to take it seriously and to succeed. And if you're off somewhere, you have to be independent, take responsibility, can't just run home to Mom and Dad.

Where're you sending Janie? Teddy asks.

Her's is a very different situation. I can't do without her just yet. She's made herself indispensable to me. Plus, I know she's serious and will finish.

She's becoming pretty indispensable to me, too, Teddy says. But the school she goes to has to be what's best for her.

The rest of the meal continues like this—polite conversation with a definite undertone of hostility. When they finish coffee and desert, Bosworth makes it clear it's time for Teddy to leave.

You can walk him to his car and say goodnight, he says, but don't linger. Hurry back in and I'll help you with the dishes. It was very nice to meet you, young Ted, he adds, the corners of his mouth twitching up into a mean smile that indicates he's won, and as Janie chastely kisses him goodnight at his car, he knows his assessment is right.

I'll try to sneak out and come see you later, she whispers.

He wants to say, I know he's molesting you. Get in the car with me now and I'll take you away from all this, but all he can manage is, Okay.

He now knows Bosworth is molesting Janie. Has to be. Hell, he treats her like a wife. What he doesn't know is what he's going to do about it—at least he didn't until Janie climbed in his window later that night.

You look at me different now, don't you? he asks her.

Would I have come over if I did?

That isn't an answer.

She stops unbuttoning her blouse to unbutton and unzip his jeans.

Wait, he says, grabbing her wrists. Stop.

You're the first guy who's ever said *that*.

How many guys you been with?

Enough to know what y'all like.

Has anybody ever . . .

What?

. . . raped you?

She shakes her head, her eyes narrowing, the crease between them looking like a cut. No. Why'd you, what made you ask that?

I don't know. I read something that says a lot of girls are—and usually by someone they know. Even a family member.

Yeah, I've heard that, too, but I've never been.

She leans in and starts kissing him again, undoing the last of her buttons, quickly unsnapping her bra, exposing her small breasts. Taking his hand, she lifts it to her left breast, and cups it.

Brian doesn't really treat you like a stepdaughter, does he?

Technically, I'm not.

You're not?

He was with my mom for a while; they weren't married. He treats you more like a . . . .

Roommate? she offers.

I was gonna say *girlfriend*.

Girlfriend? she says and laughs.

I'm gonna kill the son of a bitch, he thinks, and it isn't the first time he's thought it, but even at this point, it's still more idle thought than serious intention. That comes a few minutes later when they're having sex. She's on her back, legs spread, he's on top, hammering away, admittedly all enthusiasm and not much finesse. His ear is at her mouth and she is whispering to him, the usual stuff, Oh God, it feels so good. You're so good. Don't stop. Don't stop. And then, she begins saying something she's never said before, something that turns an idle thought into a serious intention and costs Brian Bosworth his life.

Fuck me, daddy. Fuck me, daddy. Fuck me, daddy, she says over and over again. Fuck me, daddy. Fuck me, daddy. Fuck me, daddy.

He had only ever heard two other women say that—one an actress in a porn video, the other a character in a book, both of them black—but knew it was an expression used by a lot of women who hadn't been molested and who weren't thinking about their actual dads as they said it. But something about the way she said it, something in her voice, sounded like the way she talked to *him*, something in the way her eyes were closed, the way she no longer seemed aware of him, made him want to kill Brian Bosworth.

For the rest of the night, all Teddy can think about is what Janie had said and the way she had said it. Try as he might to think of other things—*anything* else, all he can hear is her frenzied phrase over and over, all he can see is the ecstatic expression on her contorted face.

I'm gonna fuckin' kill him, Teddy says.

Mr. Thompson nods his understanding, then gives him a wide-eyed, conspiratorial expression.

If that's a serious threat, I'll have to report you to the authorities. Are you really going to kill Mr. Bosworth?

So formal, Teddy thinks. Making a threat really makes a professional out of him.

No, Teddy says.

Are you even going to hurt him?

No.

But you believe he is molesting his stepdaughter, Janie?

I know it.

Then we report it to the police, and they'll conduct an investigation. If he's guilty, they'll find out, protect Janie, and take care of the stepdad.

Fuck me, daddy. Fuck me, daddy. Fuck me, daddy.

The litany plays in Teddy's mind at the mention of the word dad. He tries to turn it off, but can't. He tries to ignore it, but it just won't stop. It's taunting, tormenting him, and he can't make it stop, can't keep it from driving him to put Bosworth in the ground, for, he thinks, that might be the only way to silence the voice.

Take care of him, Teddy says inside a harsh, cynical laugh. I know how to take care of him.

But you're not going to?

No, Mr. Thompson, Teddy says in his most robotic voice, I would never hurt another human being. I'm just telling you how it makes me feel.

You're angry?

Teddy smiles, but there's no pleasure in it. A little, *yeah*.

I'd like to refer you to someone.

I'd like to keep seeing you.

You can. And I want you to.

Thanks, Mr. Thompson.

But you need to see someone else, too. Someone more qualified to help you deal with this. I'm just a guidance counselor. This is all just a little over—

I really don't—

I insist.

Okay.

And remember what I said. Let the police handle this, Thompson says.

A couple of days pass.

A plan is hatched.

He's read enough crime novels, watched enough cop shows to know how to do it—steal a weapon, drop it when you're done, wear gloves, avoid transferring evidence, make it look random, motiveless, keep your cool, don't hesitate.

He does it during school.

It's a Thursday. Bosworth's day off.

He tells Janie he won't see her during lunch because he has to make up a test he's missed. When Bosworth comes to the school to bring Janie her lunch, Teddy slides beneath the toolbox in the back of his truck.

As soon as Bosworth pulls back into the garage of his house and the door is down, Teddy grips the small pistol he had stolen from Bosworth's own little arsenal the night before and crawls out from beneath the toolbox.

His heart is racing so fast, the blood pumping through him so rapidly, his breaths coming so quickly, he feels like he'll pass out.

Do it.

I can't.

You've got to.

Teddy starts to crawl back beneath the toolbox, to hide like the coward he is, until he can sneak out when Bosworth's not around.

What about Janie?

I just can't. I'm sorry. I just—

Fuck me, daddy. Fuck me, daddy. Fuck me, daddy.

He shoots Bosworth in the back of the head.

Just like that. One little pop and the man crumples to the floor dead.

He stands there stunned. Is he really dead? Is it really *that* easy to kill someone? He thought there'd be more to it. A lot more.

The small enclosure is filled with the acrid odor of gun powder and his ears are still ringing, but he takes a moment to shut out all that and see if the pornographic litany that's been tormenting him for the past few days is gone. If it's not, he thinks, the next person I shoot'll be me. He listens and listens, but all he hears is, Janie's got a gun. Janie's got a gun.

Yeah, and his name is Teddy.

Maybe slaying the monster actually achieved its intended end.

But is the monster really dead?

He knows he needs to leave, to get out of the garage as soon as possible, but he waits. He's scared the man is going to jump up any minute and kill him, but he doesn't seem to be breathing. Bosworth is on his stomach, head down, so he can't tell for sure, but his back and sides don't seem to be expanding and contracting.

After what seems like far too long, he slowly climbs over the tailgate and down onto the cement floor of the garage. Holding the gun out in front of him, he carefully approaches the body lying beneath the open driver's side door. When he reaches him, he pushes Bosworth over with his foot. The man is heavy—is it dead weight?—and it takes a few tries, but he finally gets him over.

His nose looks broken from hitting the door or the floor, but he looks okay otherwise—except for being dead and all.

There is very little blood.

When Teddy arrives back at school, the monster dead, the weapon at the bottom of the bay, he doesn't feel much different than before he'd left—more tired now that the tension and adrenaline are out of his body, spent from the run, relieved, glad it's over—but not a new man, not an altered person. He and his world are the same.

He sits through fifth and then sixth periods like he does every other day—until Relentless Rhonda, the school resource officer, shows up and asks to see him.

Where were you last period? she asks when they're in the empty hallway together.

The bathroom mostly, he says. I've got a virus or something.

Lean against the wall for me.

Why?

I'm gonna pat you down.

What is it?

She does.

I didn't want to do this in front of your classmates, she says, her mouth not far from his ear, as she feels his clothes for a weapon. Sorry to have to.

It's okay. What's this about?

Where'd you put the gun?

What gun?

Janie's got a gun.

Why'd you do it? she asks.

Do what?

If he's really messin' with his daughter, I mean, I understand—most people would, but there are better ways to—

What're you talking about?

You did what a lot of people would want to, but couldn't—or wouldn't. What makes one person actually do it while thousand of others would just want to?

Did someone see me? he wonders. I was so careful. How could they even—

She pulls him off the wall and leads him through the bright, wide hallway toward . . . where exactly? The principal's office? Her car? The sheriff's department?

If only Mr. Thompson would've acted a little sooner, she says.

Whatta you mean?

He didn't really think you'd do it.

Do what? Teddy says, thinking, he knew damn well I was gonna do it. Hell, he all but told me to.

He's in a meeting with your parents, the school psychologist, and the principal right now. Isn't that just . . . he was meeting with them while you were doing it. Your parents are brokenhearted. He's been watching you. When he realized you were skipping, he called Mr. Bosworth to check on him, but got no answer. We sent a deputy by to check on him, and found . . . It's killin' Mr. Thompson he didn't act sooner, but we all heard you say on the tape you wouldn't do it, that you weren't going to kill him.

What tape?

The one of your session with Mr. Thompson. We all listened as you threatened to kill Mr. Bosworth, but then we heard you say you weren't really gonna do it.

I've been set up, he thinks. The son of bitch set me up. No wonder he didn't report Bosworth. No wonder he acted so unethically. He's been playing me from the moment I stepped out of the mechanical closet with Janie, but why?

Nobody blames Mr. Thompson. He's got such a difficult job. And we're lucky to have him. He really cares about you guys. I don't know what little Janie would do without him.

You should see the way he is with her. It's a good thing they were already close.

Has he been following her? Teddy wonders. Is that why he was outside the mechanical closet when we came out? Were they already involved? Had he killed the quarterback—or gotten someone else to do it the way he got me to kill Bosworth? Was Bosworth even a pedophile?

Poor little thing, Rhonda says. Losing her dad and her boyfriend all in one day.

Teddy shakes his head. You stupid, gullible, son of a bitch.

Don't be so hard on yourself. You were way out of your league.

Without knowing it, he had been dealing with the devil, a demented, but devious pederast who'd gotten a twofer—eliminating his competition, using another competitor to do it.

As Rhonda leads him toward the front office, he turns and glances back down the hall. Students and teachers spill out of classrooms, straining to catch a glimpse of the killer. Through the windows of the office, he can see his parents; his mom shaking she's crying so hard; his dad holding her lovingly for support in the same way Thompson's holding Janie.

Fuck me, daddy. Fuck me, daddy. Fuck me, daddy.

An elbow to the teeth, fist to the gut. As Rhonda goes down, Teddy comes up with her gun.

Shouts.

Screams.

Snatching the office door open, he tackles Thompson.

Janie cries out as she's knocked down.

Teddy, his mom screams.

No, Son, stop, his dad yells. What're you doing?

Fuck me, daddy. Fuck me, daddy. Fuck me daddy.

Pandemonium.

Everybody back away.

Straddling Thompson, gun jammed beneath his chin.

You have one chance, Teddy says to him, voice low. Only one. Answer the right way and you live.

Thompson, tears streaming out the corners of his eyes, nods.

What does Janie say when you fuck her?

What?

One chance. Live or die. What does she say when you fuck her?

Thompson doesn't respond right away.

Teddy pulls back the trigger.

No answer is the wrong answer. What does she say?

She says, he starts, then stops.

What? What does she say?

She says, Fuck me, daddy. Fuck me, daddy. Fuck me, daddy.

As Teddy begins to pull the trigger, Thompson says, That's the right answer. I get to live.

It's the correct answer. I said answer the right way—which was to convince me you honestly had no idea.

Teddy pulls the trigger.

Point-blank range.

In the face.

More than once.

Fuck me, daddy. Fuck me, daddy. Fuck me, daddy.

Janie's got a gun. Whole world's come undone.

Then his mom, Honey, what have you done?

Then silence.

The Exchange

Vicious stands in the shadows and watches.
It's something he does.
People amuse him.
He even occasionally wonders what it'd be like to be one of them.

Highway intersection.
Gas station.
Two miles outside Desperation.
He's just passing through, taking rural routes, avoiding 5-0. Dubbed different names in different cities, none of them original, only one of them accurate, he's wanted for several unsolved serial killings in at least five states.

She sits in the driver's seat of a champagne-colored sedan, parked away from the pumps near the pay phones, a young teenage boy in the seat behind her.
Windows down.
Evening breeze.

Near dark.

Backlit by the last of the setting sun on the western horizon beyond.

Attractive. Stylish. Short blonde hair. Long, elegant neck. Something even in the way she sits is stately, sophisticated.

Car off, constantly scanning the two entrances of the gas station and turning to look every time headlights from another vehicle light up hers, she's obviously waiting for someone.

Not necessarily trolling for his next victim, Vicious just enjoys watching. Of course, you never know. Browsing often turns to buying.

When she's not craning in search of the person she's meeting, she's angrily punching numbers into her cell phone, waiting, then smacking the phone closed in frustration.

Continuing to scan, crane, and call, her impatience escalating. Behind her, the young teenager in the back seat remains motionless, the bony shoulders of his boyish body taut with tension.

Eventually, a dust-covered truck with magnetic lawn care signs on the doors, rakes, shovels, and hoes sticking out of the back, and a trailer with push and riding lawnmowers in tow, pulls in and parks in front of her. A tall, muscular, berry-skinned man jumps out of the driver's side door, runs around to the passenger's side and helps a little girl of about six climb down, a small cartoon-clad suitcase in one tiny hand, a partially clothed Barbie doll in the other.

Something about the child reminds Vicious of his little sister, Annabella, the recollection bringing with it cries and screams, and the accompanying images of abuse.

Sorry, Annie. Wished I could've saved you.

Grabbing a pillow, blanket, and stuffed animal, the man follows the little girl over to the car.

Look what Daddy got me, she says, as she climbs in the back seat, adding to the boy now beside her. You should've come with us.

The boy doesn't respond.

After cramming the pillow, blanket, and teddy bear into the back seat, the man squats down beside the front passenger window and says, Sorry we're late. We took a little longer at the toy store than we meant to.

The woman snatches the small suitcase from the back seat and begins to rifle through it. Just once why not act like it's just a regular Sunday instead of friggin' Christmas.

Ignoring the woman, the man looks at the boy. Hey buddy. How's it goin'? I wish you would've come.

The boy doesn't say anything.

Where are her dance shoes? the woman asks.

They're not in there? I told her to grab them right before we left the house. Turning to the little girl, who's humming as she wrestles designer clothes onto her Barbie, the man says, Sweetie, did you forget your dance shoes?

I thought you said you were gettin' 'em, Daddy, she says.

No, remember I told you to—It's okay. I'll go back and get them and bring them over later tonight.

I need to talk to you, the woman says.

Before he can respond, she's out of the car and slamming the door.

Uh-oh, the man says, but neither of his kids responds.

You forgot her goddam dance shoes on purpose, the woman says when the man joins her between their vehicles.

As the man protests his innocence, the little girl says, Daddy misses Mommy.

Without acknowledging her, the boy continues to seethe in silence.

In the background, near the edge of consciousness, the desultory nosie of traffic drifts over from the highway— the breezy, swishing sounds of approaching vehicles, deceleration, the warning thu-dumps leading up to the light, acceleration, then the fading in the distance until it falls off into nothing.

My therapist is right. You're continually committing all these passive-aggressive acts against me as if this is my fault, the woman is saying, but you're the one who couldn't keep his dick out of every skank in town.

Clinching his fists, the man steps back, as if to keep from hitting her. Turning away from her, he takes in a deep breath, and lets out a long sigh.

This isn't working, she says.

What? the man asks, as he turns back to face her, his posture and voice back in nice-guy mode. Our divorce?

All this swapping, she says. It's too disruptive.

I can take them longer, he says. Love to.

What? No. Todd doesn't want to go as it is.

He doesn't want to go anywhere, the man says. It's not just my place.

Well—

I could come home.

You really don't get it, do you? she says. There's not a word for how through we are.

As Mom and Dad continue to argue, the little girl, seemingly oblivious to it, plays with her Barbie. Todd, stone-faced and silent, sits perfectly still in the seat beside her.

I just don't have any more right now, the man is saying. You've drained me dry.
    Not *me*, she says. You haven't given me a goddam dime. It's for your kids. And if you're so broke, quit taking her to the toy store every other weekend. What kind of message does that send?
    That we're fine, he says. That we're all okay.
    She snorts and shakes her head.
    We are. Or will be.
    I'm sick of you lookin' like Santa Claus and me like the fuckin' Grinch.
    I just miss them so much.
    I'm sick of having to be the only grownup in this relationship, Steve.

Inside the car, the little girl says, You think they'll get back together?
    She says it without looking at either her parents or her brother, as if she's asking Barbie.
    Todd doesn't say anything.

Savannah says you're planning on coming to her dance recital, the woman is saying.
    Of course, Steve says.
    Do you have a ticket?
    You have our tickets, he says.
    I don't think we should sit together, she says. It's too confusing for the kids. Sends the wrong message.

The man slowly shakes his head, his look one of disbelief. You know there aren't any seats left. Why're you . . . Don't do this. Don't be that kind of woman.

Having dropped some vital part of Barbie's clothing on the floorboard, Savannah is leaning over to get it.

Suddenly, and without changing expressions, Todd hits her as hard as he can on the back with the bottom of his fist.

Vicious sees himself in the boy, and remembers more of his childhood—the torture inflicted on the boy and girl who looked like him and his sister, but had long since become different people.

Neither child had survived.

The girl was in the ground—had been for nearly two decades.

The boy had been swallowed whole by the dragon.

He glances back over at the parents. They're oblivious, too coiled up in their anger, too busy spewing their venom, to notice what it's doing to their kids.

After a small yelp when he first hits her, Savannah is now fighting back tears, sniffling as she tries to swallow her pain.

They're *my* tickets, the man is saying. I pay for the damn lessons.

I've got to go, the woman says.

She takes a step away from him, but he grabs her arm.

The *hell* you think you're doin'?

Hey, everything's okay, he says, shifting back into his nice-guy persona. It'll all work out. We'll all be fine. You'll see.

Snatching her arm away from him, she says, Don't you ever lay a goddam hand on me. Not ever.

She walks around and gets into the car. Glancing back at her kids as she starts the engine, she can see that Savannah is upset.

    What's wrong, honey? What is it?

    Nothin', Mommy. I'm fine. Everything's fine.

Pulling away from the curb, just before she rolls up the windows, the woman says, You guys want pizza?

It's dark now. The lights from the small store where the bored-looking attendant is watching a small television with bad reception are bright and intrusive. From the highway, the growing groan of a semi engine accelerating momentarily drowns out everything else. In the darkness the disembodied noise sounds hostile, menacing.

    Vicious smiles.

Vicious watches as Steve slowly pulls out of the gas station parking lot and onto the highway, then climbs into his car, flips a coin to see who he'll follow.

    Flip.
    Catch.
    Call.
    Heads the man.
    Tails the woman.
    Lifting his hand.
    Heads.

    He'll do the man first, then the woman (she won't be hard to find), killing, as he has so many times before, over and over again, his dad and his mom, punishing them for his being born, and this time, too, for what they did to Annabella.

He'll spare the kids, like he always does in these situations. What was it the Jacksonville paper had called him? It sounded like an Old West six-shooter. What was it?

He smiles as he recalls. The Orphanmaker.

The Orphanmaker will be making a couple of calls tonight, exchanging the lives Todd and Savannah would have had for existences not unlike his own. If he had any empathy, if the dragon had left behind any humanity, he'd unspring their mortal coils, too. God knows Annabella got a better deal than he did. But it's not up to him. Not really. And it hadn't been for a long time. He doesn't deal the cards. He just plays the hands.

Pillow Talk

Is there anything you haven't done with him? he asked.

They were lying naked on the hard hotel bed, but even if they hadn't been, she would have known he was talking about sex—is there anything you haven't done with him *sexually*? Sex was implied. It always was with him. She also knew that the him referred to her husband. He never used his name, only *him*.

The room was small and had that faintly unpleasant hotel smell, a blend of stale air, other people, smoke (something that was almost always present, even in nonsmoking rooms), all of which mingled with the commercial chemical odors of cleanser and bug spray. The bland uniformity and cheapness of the room was half hidden in the dusky dimness, and a single strip of light from the partially open bathroom door cut across the bed, overexposing odd parts of their bodies.

You mean sexually? she asked.

Is there anything you'll do with me you won't do with him?

She thought about all they had done. *How can you not know the answer to that question?* she wondered.

I don't do much of anything with him anymore, she said, stalling. You know that.

She loved him in an out-of-control, obsessive way, but she hated him when he was like this. Hated herself even more. Why did it have to be this way? Wasn't it possible to love something without destroying it?

Their love had started out so tender, so kind. They had been friends first. Talking for hours at a time—on the phone, in his car, in the park—him really listening, caring about what she thought and felt and had to say.

I'm not talking *do*, he said, I'm talking *have done*—as in ever.

She looked over at him, his dark, intense features, the childlike timidity and insecurity lurking just behind his burning brown eyes. She wondered if he had something specific in mind. Was this about a particular act—the only thing he had asked for that she had declined—or something else?

I've never cheated on you with him, she said.

He let out a harsh, humorless laugh. Isn't that what you do every time you go back to him? Every time you let him fuck you?

This isn't good, she thought. *How can I get out of this? Change the subject? Reassure him?* Suddenly, her skin was chilled and her nude body shivered beside his.

You can't be jealous of *Eric*, she said. How could anyone be jealous of *Eric*?

She really couldn't understand how any man could find Eric anything but sweet in a mildly amusing way, but especially *this* man. He was everything Eric wasn't. How could he be so threatened? Was it her? Something she was doing? Or just the desperate nature of adultery? Maybe their faithlessness was only making marginally worse what was really obsessive possessiveness.

Why won't you leave him? he asked. And I'm not jealous.

I've told you, she said with strained patience, it would destroy him. I couldn't do that.

But you'll destroy me? he asked. You'll do *that*?

This is *destroying* you? she asked, suddenly aware of just how self-destructive this was for them both.

This is crazy, he said. If you're not willing to leave him—if you're never going to leave him, what are we doing? You don't love me. I'm nothing to you.

You're *everything* to me, she said. I love you more than myself. Can't you see that? Surely you must know how little of me's left.

He didn't respond. She hated when he did that. She felt herself about to rush forward, her words tumbling out like paratroopers in hostile territory. It was as if she were watching from outside herself, feeling the beginnings of panic around her ragged edges, but unable to do anything about it.

There's nothing I won't do for you, she said. I've proven that over and over. How can you still wonder if you're important to me. You're more important to me than me. I'll do anything for you. You know that.

She still remembered Eric's half-puzzled, half-alarmed look when he walked in on her in the bathroom and saw that she had shaved off all her pubic hair. She had explained to him that she had just done it on a whim in the bathtub one night when she had had a little too much wine. What else could she say? My boyfriend asked me to do it, said he wanted to see what it looked like, what it felt like when he went down on me.

With the awkwardness and excitement of an adolescent, Eric had exclaimed, You've got no pussy.

Strictly speaking, that's not true, she had said.

You look like you've just had an operation or something, he had said.

But he was wrong. It was the first thing to come to his mind, but only because he didn't quite know what else to say. Actually, had Eric known more, had he been a different sort of man, he would have known what she really looked like was sex—unvarnished, raw, razor-burned sex. Her boyfriend could see and get to her better this way, which was why she could put up with the prickly, itchy, rash-like skin that reappeared beneath her panties every few days. And while all this may or may not be true, she knew the real reason he had asked her to do it. It was to see if she would, to see if she were truly his, and in the process mark her as his own. She was and she did and he had. But, of course, it wasn't enough. It never was.

You'll do anything for me except leave him, he said, lying perfectly still beside her in the darkening room.

What do I have to do to convince you that I love you? she asked.

He shook his head. I know you love me, he said, a new edge of defensiveness in his voice. Never mind. Just forget the whole thing.

What whole thing? she asked, her pulse a lump in her throat.

He didn't say anything.

You talking about this conversation? she asked. Or us?

He shrugged.

She felt him retreating, returning to sea like the tide, felt herself losing him. Suddenly, she felt all alone, desperation growing in her like a rapidly spreading disease.

He jumped up from the bed and began to dress.

Please don't do this, she pleaded. I love you. I've done everything you've ever asked me to.

She thought about how she had not only let him talk dirty to her, calling her the sorts of names her mama taught her not to let anyone, but also saying the things he wanted to hear, even though she sometimes felt silly and guilty for saying them. She had shaved, she had swallowed, she had let him come on her stomach and breasts and face. She had let him tie her up and spank her. She had danced for him, masturbated for him, and inserted various objects in her body for him. She had peed on him and let him pee on her, even though she didn't get any pleasure out of either activity. She had been his bad little school girl, his horny French maid, his nympho boss, her breasts barely restrained by her business suit. They had done every position—*every*thing, with one exception, and yet he was dressed and heading toward the door.

What do you want from me? she asked, really wanting to know.

She wasn't especially repressed. It wasn't the things she had done for him that bothered her so much (hell, she enjoyed most of them). It was why she was doing them. She could enjoy them more if they weren't acts of desperation, weren't sacrifices of herself to the demon-god inside him that could never be appeased.

You, he said. All of you.

What had happened to them? They hadn't started out like this. There had been genuine love, real consideration. When had they entered this widening gyre? Why couldn't the center hold? How could something so powerful be so fucking fragile?

You have me, she said. Every single cell.

But so does he, he said. Nothing is truly, uniquely mine. Ours.

I am, she said, and the desperation in her voice made her nauseated.

I love you, he said. I'm sorry for loving you so much. I wish I could have . . . I'll pay for the room as I leave. Stay as long as you like. I'm sorry. I'm so sorry for everything. I wish I could be different.

Turning, placing his hand on the doorknob, she blurted out, Eric and I have never done that thing you asked me to do.

God, she couldn't even say it.

He stopped, letting go of the knob, turning to face her. He didn't have to ask what thing. He knew.

Never? he asked.

She shook her head, unable to speak.

Why not?

I didn't want to, she said. Not with him.

But you do with me? he asked.

Of course not, she thought. Who would really want a—then she thought of how many people, men and women, did it every day. Maybe some people do, she reconsidered. Or maybe they don't have many other options or have something to prove . . . like I do now.

I do, she said, her voice quavering slightly.

Have you ever done it with anyone?

No, she said emphatically, her revulsion showing.

But you will with me? he asked.

She would. She would pay the enormous price it would cost her, fully aware of its futility. She loved him after all, and there was nothing left of her anyway.

If you'll never wonder again if I love you, she said.

He shook his head in a mixture of disbelief and admiration. I never will.

Okay then, she said.

Walking over to the bed, he knelt down beside it, as if almost bowing before her with admiration and appreciation.

You're sure? he asked. I don't want you to if you don't want to.

Will you know I love you even if we don't? she asked.

He hesitated. I will, he said. Just your willingness was enough.

If it truly is, then I'd rather not, she said. But if that's what it takes to convince you that I'm yours, that I love you like no other person alive, then I will.

It's fine, he said. Really. You don't have to.

Maybe not right now, she thought, but one day and soon this would come up again. Eventually she would have to do it. And she would. She would destroy herself to convince him of her love, that he was safe to love her, but then, of course, there would be nothing left of her to love.

The Day of Undoing

He doesn't realize what day it is.
     The thought arrives unbidden.
     Intrusive.
     Inconvenient.
     Bent over the bed, Abbey has been attempting to think of nothing in particular, only to be mindful, alert to signs of arousal, sensitive to sensation, aware of every breath, and open, in ways obvious and not, to all possibilities. Now, her attention is off her body and what Blake is doing to it and on her thoughts.
     Kneeling behind her, phallus in his hand, he works his way up her legs one at a time, his tongue leaving a winding path of moisture.
     One thought can change so much.
     Of course, it's never just one thought. With her, thought follows thought in a compulsive consecution. At times, she even thinks about thinking, cognizant of her thoughts themselves, as if separate from them, observing them with interest from a place apart. This particular phenomenon of self-consciousness most often occurs in moments like this one

when she's trying to have no thoughts at all. It's why her experiences with meditation have been so frustrating. Beginners mind isn't possible for a mind like hers.

Blake is happy to have his wife back—particularly because her return has brought with it a new amenability to his appetites, perhaps even a few yearnings of her own.

She can't see what he's doing, of course, but she can hear it and feel it, the wet rhythmic motions, the rise and fall of which coincides with the beat of his breathing.

His tongue has reached its destination now, lightly caressing the delicate folds of flesh, the tip of his nose touching the little pink rose above, neither of which are without delectation, but at times his attention becomes so concentrated on himself that he loses focus on her, and then his face is just there, passively pressed up against her moist, most intimate parts. It's not a selfish gesture, just a momentary lapse in concentration—which he has far less than she does when their rolls are reversed. Not nearly as coordinated as he, she finds it difficult just to rub herself and him simultaneously for more than a moment at a time.

He knows what to do with his tongue, knows what she likes.

Soft.
Slow.
Musical.
Aggressive.
Playful.
Variety.
She likes variety.

The tip of his tongue gently pushes against the upper folds to find and encircle the small singularity of her sex. As it swells, he takes it between his lips with the slight sucking sound of a child trying to whistle, and a shudder runs through her, a powerful ripple emanating outward from that one small point.

She shifts her weight slightly, and the bed, their bed, lets out a small creak.

Their bed holds the history of their marriage the way their bodies bear the lines of their lives.

This increasingly too-small double bed is a battlefield for their many skirmishes, verdant garden for most of their sexual entanglements, counselor's couch for the plethora of therapies they attempt to administer—all that unsolicited advise offered and rejected.

Here, they talk til the first glow of false dawn and remain silent for days on end, refusing to offer even the most rudimentary words of courtesy. Here, too, they make love and fuck, whisper and yell, laugh and cry. On these materials—cloth, wood, metal—they have been their sickest (once simultaneously when they both had the stomach flu and spent an entire Sunday taking turns vomiting), and experienced their greatest healings.

Here they toss and turn, sleep and feel the frustration of insomnia, read, work, write, watch, and dream. It was here he found her clit, she, truly discovered his cock, and each what made the other come. No one else had ever slept in this bed, and they had only as a couple. It had been their first purchase five years ago after combining their checking accounts and moving in together.

Two year ago, when she had been thirty and he, thirty-one, and they had decided it was time for children, it had been this bed that hosted their earnest attempts at conception—as well as the tears that dampened her pillow each month she got her period. It was in this bed that she finally did conceive. It had been this bed that had received her tears of joy, this bed she was consigned to when the spotting began, and it was this bed he had helped her into when she returned from her D & C after the miscarriage.

It is utterly and uniquely theirs, this bed he has her bent over.

She breaths in deeply, but quietly, trying not to distract him.

The room smells of fresh paint and old wood soaked with oil soap, and she finds it unfamiliar and sad. Unpacked boxes are scattered through every room of the rented house, and because it is not theirs the way their bed is, their bed seems as out of place in it as she does.

Why are we here? What was I thinking?

She knows the answers to both questions—the real reasons, not just the ones given to family and friends, not just the ones they admit to each other. Sure, her new job is a great opportunity—one that will provide him with opportunities of his own—and the small north Florida coastal town will no doubt be a pleasant change. But in her most honest moments, she must admit, at least to herself, that had she not miscarried or felt the need to attempt to save her marriage one more time, she would not be here now, bent over her old bed, in an alien house in this small town with the depressing name in the state of Denial.

Her previous attempt to save her marriage had been sexual. And it worked. She had felt Blake's restlessness as a warning that he was about to go in search of something new, something different, exotic, so she gave it to him, became every woman, and he was so grateful that, for a while at least, he only had eyes for her. It didn't last, of course. Nothing does. But uprooting her entire life and attempting to transplant it in the sandy soil of Florida was not that much more extreme than becoming—what was the term he used?—a freak in the sheets.

It occurs to her that many people move to Florida to die.

She wonders if, rather than taking root, her marriage will be buried in the salty sand that seems only capable of sustaining sea oats and palm trees.

She's not sure how she feels about that possibility. She's only just now beginning to feel again, as if regaining consciousness, but not completely resurfaced from the underworld, and she's still not feeling much of anything.

Blake thinks she's back, finally emerging from the dark place she went following the miscarriage, and she is, just not as all the way back as he thinks—or hopes. Like a shell-shocked soldier returning from war, she appears to have come home, but in some ways she never will.

When she first lost her baby—others may think of it as a fetus, and maybe that's all it was, but to her it was her little Elizabeth—she felt such guilt. It had been as if she had split into two parts—a pitiless cop and a guilt-ridden criminal. Her cop self interrogated her criminal self relentlessly. Why had she murdered her child? Had she not really wanted her? How had she done it? Too much exercise? Too much wine? Too much worry? Too much conflict with Blake? Too much stress at work? Why hadn't she taken better care of herself and the precious gift she had been given? Had this been her way of punishing Blake? Why all this repressed hostility toward him? Was it all because he made her submit, because of all the different ways he had fucked this staunch feminist?

At first, she wanted to get pregnant again right away, then she never wanted to make another attempt. She tried to assure herself that it was for the best, nature or God or random blind fucking luck that she didn't have a child that would spend its short life in pain, but soon there was just the demon, the not unfamiliar depressant that had become her dearest companion. Hello, Darkness, my old friend.

Everyone had been so happy she was finally pregnant. Her folks had waited and hoped and prayed so long. Her friends and colleagues were happy, too. She really *could* have it all. She was the embodiment of post-modern feminism.

For a while immediately following her miscarriage, people still asked after the baby, when she was due, where she was registered, what she needed. She even found herself in the baby section of department stores, gazing glassy-eyed at the blurry images of lacy outfits and carved wooden furniture, her cheeks streaked moist and salty.

It was little wonder she went to such a dark place. What was far more curious, especially to her, was how she ever floated to the surface again. How had she survived the darkest of dark nights of the soul? She couldn't explain it. But its bafflingness had opened her up to the possibility of a whole new life—one with transcendence.

This new openness and hope had caused her to once again open herself up to Blake and to be willing, perhaps even anxious, to begin her new journey.

Reminding herself to stop thinking, she returns her attention to Blake.

Having abandoned her singularity, his tongue, wet with her, has made the short journey to the pink blossom of her bottom. No wonder she's been distracted. What he's doing now, he's doing for himself. Not that it didn't hold a pleasure all its own for her, too—he had shown her that; it never would have occurred to her—but she needed to be highly aroused already or optimally be simultaneously stimulated. Of course, she could reach down and finish the job he had started, but she just didn't have it in her at the moment.

This isn't what she wants.

She wants to make love, nurture and nourish each other. It's what she needs, what she had been hoping for.

Her self-awareness works its way to the fore again, and she thinks about the rawness of the language they use, the coarseness of their sex acts—when had this become the norm for them? The words and actions themselves weren't of concern. They weren't new. And she no longer heard the FemiNazi voice of disapproval she once had. What concerns her is their commonness, their omnipresence. When had it become this way and why? One word comes immediately to mind.

Porn.

The ubiquity of porn in popular culture, his use of it, her acceptance and occasional participation, is impacting their relationship more than she had previously realized. Sure, he had always used porn. It isn't porn itself, but the type and volume and her acceptance of it that's the difference.

When she first discovered his use of porn, back when it was mostly the magazines that now seemed so mild, it had hurt her a little that he would want to look at any woman but her. It wasn't an issue of cheating or betrayal; she just didn't like to think she wasn't enough.

As a feminist, she was disturbed by the obvious exploitation of the young girls with augmented bodies, open mouths, spread legs. And they were girls—too young, too inexperienced, too powerless to be in a position to truly have a choice about what they were doing.

Eventually, slowly and not without some residual guilt, she became more open to a certain type of porn for herself occasionally and for whatever and whenever he wanted for himself—especially after she lost the baby. And porn was not without its benefits—as an aid to arousal, an enhancement of experience, an answer to insatiability that kept him home and STD-free.

But now she realizes porn is doing something else to their relationship. It's masculinizing their sexual interactions. It is making it experimental and—what? not clinical exactly, but purely physical—mechanical. They were at the verge of having soulless sex.

She likes to fuck, even to be fucked, but she also likes to make love, and that's something they no longer do. How long had it been since their souls had kissed? She can't remember.

Blake doesn't realize what's happening any more than he knows what day it is. He's still kind to her, still her sensitive boy, but there's more of an edge to him now, and he seems less integrated, compartmentalizing his life, detaching himself as much from her as the rest of the world. It's partly his obsessions, his fear of dying in obscurity, but there's more to it than that.

The tip of his tongue darts in, then out. In and out. In and out. His breathing through his nose intensifies, its warmth drying the wetness he has left. He moans and the movement of his hand increases.

No. This is not what she wants right now. Stop. Don't do this. Make love to me.

She's losing him. He's losing her. They're losing something sacred.

So much loss, so much pain—the pain of squandered possibility, of stillborn potential.

This is the day for it, she thinks, as a solitary tear trickles down her cheek. He may be unaware of what day it is, but she's not. She's acutely aware, and probably will be for the rest of her life, for today is her due date.

Tables

Sitting across from Blake, Abbey begins to think about all the tables that had been between them over the years. This has never occurred to her before, and it's funny that it should now, but the distraction will do her good.

They had met at a library table in college. And though not technically love at first sight, there was a certain something. Sparkage of a kind. Both excited about their chosen fields of study, they talked incessantly, only a small portion of their words an attempt to impress or woo the other.

    She smiles to herself now at what enthusiasts they had been. How embarrassing, and yet she envies them their fire.

    Can you envy yourself? Seems strange, but Older Abbey envies Younger Abbey.

    Of course, Older Abbey doesn't wish to be Younger Abbey again.

While they were dating, they had often sat with other students on and around the weathered and chipped cement tables on the campus green, its peeling white paint clinging to their faded jeans.

Politics, religion, popular culture, books, film, even God had been the subjects of heated debates by the young lions roaring against their pathetic and passionless parents, the way, because of them, everything was so fucked.

They had held hands and shoved cake into each other's mouths around the tiny round table that held their beautiful, but tasteless wedding cake. She thought back to the kids in their wedding photos she no longer recognized.

It's so strange that he looks just the same to me today as he did then. It's only in pictures that she really catches a glimpse of how much they've changed, are changing, and how quickly the pages of their lives are yellowing.

There had been the wobbly, hand-me-down dining table his parents had given them for their apartment, her early attempts at cooking, the enormous amount of takeout they had eaten on it. It had also been on that table she had placed her typewriter when she first dared to attempt to be the writer she had always been afraid to admit she wanted to be.

Even now, she is suffused with a warmth that tingles to her fingertips and toes as she thinks about him sitting across from her reading her work, ripping each new page from the machine the moment she reached the bottom.

There had been the square and round and rectangular tables of a thousand different restaurants, of course, the meals intimate and inimitable in their intensity, preludes to movies and sexual interludes, and, eventually, going home and falling asleep in front of the TV.

Not all tables had been between them. She had been on one of them. He had stood next to her while she had her D & C, holding her hand, wiping her tears, promising a different outcome on their next attempt.

As each of them found success, their living spaces had changed, and so, too, had the tables within them. Big, solid, expensive, their kitchen table no longer wobbled. And now they also had a breakfast nooker, perpetually piled with manuscript pages, newspapers, random mail, and bills in need of paying.

Now, too, they had a formal dining room and a formal dining room table to go with it, where at Thanksgiving they gathered together to ask the Lord's blessings with family and friends. She thinks about last Christmas, the meal, the wine, the conversation, and how close they are to this Christmas.

This makes her think of how quickly every second has sped by.

All the tables and all they held and all the two of them had ever said and done and shared around them was but a blink, a single brilliant, but brief moment, now gone except in memory, soon gone forever.

Our all too brief history in tables.

This led, of course, to the table that separates them now. It's solid and polished and expensive, and, as soon as she signs her name, the very last one that will ever be between them.

The Hunt

He was still inside her the first time his phone rang, her saying something about them getting out of Desperation before it was too late.

They often talked during sex—not continually, but intermittently, comfortably, between more intense periods of groping, thrusting, and moaning. It had been that way even during their first time in her car when they were both so cold and nervous their words came out as stuttered bursts between chattering teeth. In fact, that's how Blake had come to think of sex with Brooke—coitus and conversation.

People around here are dead inside, she said. Walking around like fuckin' zombies.

Doesn't mean *we* have to be.

It's inevitable, she said. Kind of a slow suicide of the soul.

Suicide by small town, he said with a laugh. But you're not like that. Think about how many people you help.

They were in Room 6 of the Dixie Land Inn, a small, rundown roadside motel on Highway 66 a few miles outside of town. The rooms of the Dixie Land had only two things going for them, and they just happened to be the two things that mattered most to Blake and Brooke. They were clean and they were private.

You really hate this place that much? he asked.

Don't you?

Not at the moment.

If you could be anywhere in the world right now, where would it be?

Inside you.

She put her hands on his butt cheeks and pulled him toward her raising her pelvis. You're sweet, but if you could be inside me anywhere in the world where would it be?

Anywhere's just fine.

He was being honest. He didn't like Desperation any more than she did, but it was hard to think about it while he was still inside her. It was the best feeling of his life, and, as fate would have it, he had only ever felt it in Desperation.

The other reason he didn't like talking about leaving was that he knew they couldn't. Even if she could leave her husband, which he felt was doubtful when it came down to it, he couldn't let her. Thornton had been his friend since kindergarten, and though they weren't close now, he couldn't let her leave him. Losing her would devastate him, but losing his six year-old son, Zach, would kill him.

I'm serious, she was saying. We gotta get out.

We couldn't do that to Thornton.

Thornton Wyatt had peaked in high school. He was the handsome, charming, country boy quarterback and homecoming king. And even given all that, he was nice to everyone, a genuinely good person. Blake loved Brooke way back then, but a bookish, artistic, intellect couldn't compete with the Friday night super hero.

Just before prom, Brooke found out she was pregnant. She and Thornton had married right out of school. They lost that baby, but Zach came along a few years later. While Blake was off at college, Thornton got a job at the gun and pawn shop, put on a hundred pounds, and spent much of his time talking about his glory days. Now, nearing the tenth high school reunion, Thornton lived for two seasons—football and hunting. He was still a nice good ol' boy, living a small town life, something that was killing his wife.

Thornton's happy, she said. This kind of place was made for the Thornton Wyatts of the world.

Though situated on the Gulf of Mexico with its beautiful beaches and spectacular sunsets, the paper mill kept Desperation, Florida, small, its residents largely Deep South hicks who loved the thousands of acres of pine forests, river swamps, and deep woods far more than the sand and sea.

Still, he wouldn't recover.

They stopped talking and started more earnestly making love.

Blake Stacy had moved from Desperation to Gainesville to attend the University of Florida. He earned a degree in journalism and an MFA in creative writing. He had been working as a reporter for the *Miami Herald* and working on his second novel, his first having been published by a university press to critical acclaim but popular failure, when he got the call that his dad had been injured in a mill accident and needed him to come home. He hadn't been home long when he saw Brooke again. She was the home healthcare nurse assigned to his dad. Almost instantly, they fell in love and into bed. Now that his dad had died, the only thing keeping him in Desperation was Brooke.

You've got to go, she said. Even if you won't take me.

I told you I'm right where I want to be.

She managed a smile.

His phone rang again. It never rang, and now it had rung twice in the last few minutes.

You better answer that, she said. Somebody really needs to talk to you.

For a while he had hoped every call was the *Herald* wanting him back or an agent or editor who had read something he wrote wanting to read something else, but he hadn't even thought about that in a very long time. Maybe Brooke was right. Maybe this town was killing him.

I wasn't really planning on coming out of you for several more hours.

I'm not going anywhere.

He slipped out of her, hopped off the bed, and grabbed his phone off the dresser.

When he looked at the digital readout, he didn't recognize the number. He was tempted to let voice mail get it, but curiosity got the better of him.

A few minutes later, when he got back into bed, he didn't get back inside her. He couldn't. He no longer had an erection.

What is it? she asked. Who was it?

Thornton.

She sat up and pulled the covers up over her breasts.

Thornton? she said. What did *he* want?

Do you think he knows?

What'd he say?

He wants me to go hunting with him tomorrow.

What?

Yeah, he said. He was quite insistent. Haven't spoken more than a dozen words to each other in ten years, and now it's real important that we go hunting together in the morning.

You can't go with him.

I have to.

What if—

What?

A few years ago, a soldier home from Iraq went hunting with his brother and accidentally shot him.

I heard about it.

Talk around town was that it wasn't an accident, she said. Soldier found out his brother was a pedophile. Touched one of his kids or something.

You think Thornton thinks I'm a pedophile? he asked.

She laughed. I'm serious, she said. Whatta we do?

Go home, he said. Talk to him. Try to find out what he knows, what he's up to, then call me.

God, Blake, she said. If anything happened to you . . .

Let's make sure nothing happens to any of us, he said.

After Blake left the room, Brooke ran herself a hot bath, poured a stress-relieving Seamoss Hydrosoak in, and slipped her spent body, still smelling of Blake, down into the water and closed her eyes to think.

She didn't do this often, and she always felt a little guilty about not rushing back to pick up Zach from daycare, but sometimes she just needed a little more time to prepare herself to return to her life. Of course, all she could think about today was what would happen between Thorn and Blake and if her life was about to get better or far worse.

She couldn't think of Thorn without thinking of herself. Back in school, they had been *the* couple—prom king and queen, Mr. and Mrs. DHS, homecoming king and queen, most attractive, most likely to succeed. Their lives had held such promise, so many possibilities. Now look at them. They were the walking dead living dead-end lives in Desperation.

Thorn was to blame for that—most of it anyway. Not only had he let himself go, but he was holding her back, stifling her creativity, depleting her in every way.

In school, she had starred in a number of plays and musicals produced by the drama club. Everyone agreed she had real talent, and as soon as graduation rolled around, she was stage or screen bound. She couldn't decide between New York or LA, Broadway or Hollywood, but she just knew she was meant to strut and fret her hour upon the stage—sound stage or theater stage, it didn't matter.

None of it mattered now. She never got her shot, and it was Thorn's fault. Now, she was a home healthcare nurse in order to put food on the table because the best her husband could do was an hourly wage, job fit for a high school student. And wasn't that the problem? They may have given him a diploma, but he had never left high school.

Later that afternoon, Blake did something he couldn't remember ever having done. He stopped by Desperation Pawn and Gun.

The shop, which was painted toilet bowl blue, was in an old convenience store building, security bars covering the plate glass windows and double doors. Inside, on random and makeshift shelves, the stolen property of crack heads and meth addicts gathered dust in what looked to be a trailer park yard sale.

The ratty boxes of old movies on VHS were stacked on shelves next to tattered paperbacks, cassette tapes, CDs, antiquated video games, and a few DVDs with movie rental store stickers still on them. Across from them, VCRs, old gaming systems, boom boxes, and stereo systems so old they had record players in them sat in a jungle of vine-like cords and cables next to power tools and small household appliances.

Unlike the pawn part of the store, the handguns displayed in showcases and riffles in the racks that ran the length of the wall behind them were pristine, each firearm lovingly cared for until the right owner came along.

Josh Murphy, the high school senior and part-time helper, was behind the showcase carefully cleaning a stainless steel .357 on top of an old oil-stained t-shirt laid out on the counter. As usual, he wore camouflage clothing and a baseball cap, a dip of snuff making the turgid skin beneath his lip look tumorous. He was talking to Bo John, an elderly retired football coach who was sitting on a stool in front of the counter—one of many, as if this were a bar instead of a sporting goods store.

When Blake reached the two men, he stood for a while waiting for them to stop talking and acknowledge him, but it didn't happen.

Do they know? he wondered. Has Thornton already told them?

Finally, Blake said, Thornton around?

Nah, Josh said. He's out. I help you with somethin'?

You know when he'll be back?

Might be a while, he said. I'm pretty sure he's out following that hot as hell little wife of his. Goddam, she's a pretty little son of a bitch. Way too hot for Thorn, and he knows it.

Why's he following her?

Josh looked up from his gun for the first time, his narrow-eyed expression questioning Blake's IQ. Tryin' to find out who's dickin' her.

He thinks she cheating on him?

Have you seen her? he asked. Have you seen him? *I* think she is. How could she not be? Hell, I'd sure as shit dip my wick in her, she'd let me—and Thorn wouldn't shoot me.

Shoot you?

Thorn's one of the nicest sons a bitches I know, he said. He really is, but mess with his family, and blood will be shed. Make no mistake about it. I just wonder if he's gonna put the bitch down or just blow the pecker off her boyfriend.

Hell, Bo John added, he's so depressed, he might shoot his damn self.

I'm supposed to go hunting with him tomorrow—

That's *you*? Josh said, putting the gun down on the counter top and studying Blake.

Yeah, he said, and I don't have a gun.

He'll have one you can use.

I want one of my own, he said. Like that one.

Josh looked down at the .357. What you gonna hunt with that?

I'm terrified of snakes, Blake lied. I'd feel better if I had something to shoot them with.

Josh shook his head. There's a waiting period on all handguns.

Oh, Blake said. Can I rent one?

Rent? Josh said in a burst of laughter. 'Course you can't rent no gun.

Either of you got one I could borrow? he said. Just for tomorrow. I've just really got a phobia about snakes.

They both shook their heads.

Thorn'll take care of you, Josh said. Don't worry about a thing.

That night, Blake tried Brooke's cell several times but only got her voice mail, and as it got later, he regretted that her phone would show so many missed calls from his number. Did Thornton have her phone? Was she okay? Had he used one of his hundreds of guns on her before turning it on himself? As he began to panic, he realized just how much he loved her. It wasn't just an affair, not just about the amazing sex. He wanted to spend the rest of his life with her, wanted to be the one to save her.

Not sure exactly what to do, he jumped in his car and drove over to their house. He didn't know what'd he say or how he could justify showing up so late—or at all; they weren't that kind of friends. Hell, they weren't really any kind of friends any longer—but he knew he had to.

Thornton answered the door. He looked dressed for bed in sweatpants and a t-shirt, but didn't appear to have been asleep.

Blake?

Can I come in?

Sorry, he said, stepping aside.

The two men walked into the small living room, Blake scanning the house for any signs of violence.

Sorry it's so late, Blake said. Were you in bed?

Nah, he said. Brooke and Zach are. I was just catching a few highlights on *SportCenter* before I go up.

There were still signs of the handsome, athletic boy Thornton had been beneath his thinning blond hair and distant blue eyes, but they were getting buried deeper and deeper—and not just because of the excess weight. Though he rarely smiled anymore, his teeth were still snow-white, and dimples formed in his puffy cheeks.

I went by the shop today to talk to you, but they said you were out.

Yeah, I had to set some traps.

As Thornton glanced at highlights, Blake tried to see the landing at the top of the stairs and beyond into the bedrooms, but it was just too far and too dim.

The house was nice enough, clean, and it smelled good, but it looked to be furnished largely from items pawned and decorated from the thin, cheap catalogs of the type passed around at parties where the country collection, mostly candles and imitation brass butterflies, was featured on every page.

Looking around the simple, bland house, Blake felt a heavy sadness descend upon him. This was no life for Brooke. She was so beautiful, so talented, had always has such big dreams. No wonder she wanted him to get her out of here. She was trapped in a purgatory of obscurity boarding on oblivion, and if she didn't get out soon, she never would. She had been trying to tell him, but he hadn't really been listening. He had been too satisfied just being inside her that he didn't realize that something inside her was missing.

What'd you need to see me about? Thornton asked.

I'm a little apprehensive about going hunting in the morning, he said. I don't even have a gun. I've never done much of it, as you know, and I'm sure I'll just slow you down.

Thornton waved off what Blake had just said. It'll be fun. I've got a gun you can use.

Why'd you invite me?

I need to talk to you about something, he said. Something important.

Why don't we talk now?

I've got to show you something, too, he said. Come on, man. I'd really appreciate it.

Okay, okay, Blake said. Zach going with us?

Nah. Just be men tomorrow, he said. Now let's get some sleep so we'll be ready.

When Blake got to his car, he found a note from Brooke scrawled on a piece of printer paper. It read: B, Be very careful. He's up to something. Protect yourself and if comes to it, don't hesitate. I couldn't live without you. I love you. Yours, B

The sun was just cresting over the hem of pine-tree lined horizon, as Thornton turned off the rural highway onto a recently graded dirt road, the cab of the large truck vibrating as the tires passed over the tiny ruts in the hard clay.

Blake sipped on coffee Thornton had brought for him. Through the speaker in the passenger door, he could hear the sounds of barely audible country music coming from the radio. His University of Florida windbreaker was buttoned to the top, but he still shook.

I thought we were going to your lease, Blake said.

Nah, Thornton said. Too crowded. Besides, I got something special for you. I told you.

Where *are* we going?

You'll see, he said.

Blake couldn't help but wonder if his life was about to end.

It can't, he thought. I haven't done enough with it.

He was still relatively young and had always felt like he had plenty of time, that eventually things would come together, his hard work would pay off and he would finally be a successful novelist. That day had yet to come, and the longer it took to arrive, the more he questioned whether or not it ever would. But he wanted the chance to find out, wanted to live long enough to see if he might be published again and to see if he might be one of those rare writers who achieve both critical and commercial success.

He also wanted Brooke in his life.

I can't die now, he thought. I just got her. We've just started our . . . What? Journey?

What did you want to talk to me about? Blake asked.

You'll see.

They rode along in silence for a while longer, the truck bouncing along the unpaved road.

How're things at the shop?

Good, Thornton said. Always be better, but I got no big complaints.

What about at home? Blake said, attempting to sound casual, nonchalant.

Whatta you mean?

With your family, he said. How's your family?

He shrugged and shook his head. Can only speak for me, he said. I love my family and would do anything for them. Anything.

You think maybe Desperation's gettin' to Brooke? Blake asked.

What? he asked, glancing over at him, furrowing his thick brow. Whatta you . . . what does that mean? Brooke's lived here her whole life.

You know, small town, stink of the paper mill. It's a pretty depressing place.

You really think so? I love it. It's like heaven. I wouldn't want to live anywhere else in the world. Where else would you have the woods and the beaches, the rivers, lakes, and the Gulf?

Yeah, but you don't think Brooke gets bored?

What're you trying to say?

I don't know. Remember how in high school everybody said we'd see her on the big screen one day?

What keeps *you* here now? Thornton asked.

Blake shrugged. I can write from anywhere, but I probably won't be here much longer.

When Thornton smiled, Blake felt a shiver slither its way up his spine.

As Thornton unloaded the truck, Blake watched him closely, looking for tells that might reveal his plan. They were as deep in the woods as Blake had ever been. Whatever happened, he would be alone in it.

It had been a mild winter so far as this sunny January day demonstrated, and the woods, though not summer-verdant were unusually thick and green.

They had driven down an old two-trail logging path and were now in a thick river swamp; large live oaks, tall, thick-bodied pines, and ancient gnarled and twisted cypress trees surrounded them for miles and miles in every direction. Between the bases of the trees and beneath the canopy of their branches, the floor of the forest was covered with lush low-growing fern-like plants perfect for concealing snakes and small animals.

Though the sun was up, the temperature was not, and Blake realized what a mistake the UF windbreaker had been. He had chosen it because it was bright orange and blue, but warm it was not. His shoes were inadequate, too. Unlike Thornton's thick, insulated boots, Blake had on old tennis shoes.

I see you didn't bring any dogs, Blake said. Are we gonna be in stands?

Don't have stands out here, he said. We'll just walk around. See what we can see.

Isn't that dangerous?

Thornton didn't answer him, just continued to load his vest with ammunition.

Okay, Thornton said. Ready?

I need a gun, Blake said.

Thornton turned and looked at him, then looked back at the truck.

Oh, shit, man, I forgot, he said. I had two at the shop cleaned and ready to go. Damn it.

Brooke was right. Josh was right. Thornton had brought him out here to kill him and make it look like an accident.

You didn't bring me—

I guess I forgot to throw them in my truck before I left yesterday, he said. I left early and—

You brought me out here to hunt without a gun? Blake said.

Sorry, man, he said. Let me think.

They were silent a moment, Blake becoming more aware of the morning sounds of the woods—birds chirping, squirrels scampering along branches, dew dripping off trees, the quiet, airy sound of openness.

Thornton saw Blake looking around and smiled at him. Isn't it amazing out here?

Blake nodded. What'd you want to show me?

We'll get to that, Thornton said, then looked around, seeming to be considering their options. It'd take too long to drive back to the shop. By the time we got back out here it'd be nearing midday.

I'll just sit in the truck, Blake said. I'm freezing anyway, and my shoes aren't snake-proof.

Nah, man, I can't let you do that, Thornton said. I got it. You can help me and what we bag will be both of ours. Then we can have our talk. There's a big buck out here that's been eluding me. Driving me crazy. You can help me get him. We'll have him mounted, and you can hang him on your wall.

Thornton, you obviously didn't bring me out here to hunt, Blake said. I don't even have a gun. What are we doing out here really?

I told you, he said. I need to talk to you, but first—help me get the big buck. He's usually in that stand of hardwood over there. I want you to go on the other side of it and make some noise and then walk toward me. Flush him out.

You want me to walk toward you as you shoot in my direction?

You've got that bright orange jacket on—and here take this.

Thornton handed him a bright orange hunting cap.

Just make yelping noises and walk in that direction, Thornton said. I'll be over there waiting.

You're sure about this? Blake asked. Sure you want to do this?

Handing him a small VHF marine radio, he said, Turn it to channel nine so we can stay in touch. You're gonna love this. It'll be great.

I see him, Blake lied into his radio. He's about twenty feet in front of me. I'm walking toward him. We should both be headed in your direction. It won't take us long to get there. Be careful. Don't shoot me.

Never having gone near the thicket, Blake had circled back and was now trying to get behind Thornton. He could see the camper shell of the truck about fifty feet away. He had to be getting close.

I'm in position, Thornton said. Send that big bastard to me.

We should be coming out of the thicket soon, Blake said. Be watching.

I am. I'm ready.

I bet you are, you hick son of a bitch, Blake thought. Can't believe you brought me out here to kill me.

As Blake neared the area where Thornton said he would be, he found the highest point and looked around, but he couldn't see him.

Okay, he's running right toward you, Blake said into the radio. I'm chasing him. Wait. Wait. He darted in a different direction. Don't shoot. Don't shoot. I'm still in front of you, but he's—

The blast of Thornton's shotgun echoed through the woods. Then another one, and another one—not only confirming Blake's suspicions, but alerting him to his position.

Turning off his radio, he ran toward the area where the shots had been fired from. A minute later, he ran up behind Thornton, who spun toward the movement, gun raised. Blake grabbed the shotgun, stepped back, aimed and fired two shots. One missed. One hit Thornton in the chest.

Thornton fell to the ground, blood soaking his shirt, oozing out of the bullet hole in his jacket, a perplexed expression on his face.

When Blake came over and looked down at him, he felt a wave of nausea churning his stomach, bile rising in the back of his throat.

I'm shot, Thornton said between gasps, obviously in shock. Get help. Quick. No, wait. Don't leave me.

Did you think you had shot me? Blake asked.

Huh? he asked, seemingly genuinely confused. I'm shot. I got hit. What happened? Why'd—

You tried to shoot me.

Thornton's face was contorted in pain, his labored breathing coming between sighs and moans. What? No. You shot me.

After you tried to shoot me.

I didn't shoot anywhere close to you, Thornton said, pausing to gasp. Sorry I scared you—and scared the deer away . . . but a wild boar rushed me, and I had to shoot him.

Thornton's weakening eyes rolled up and to the right and Blake followed their direction to see a large black boar on the ground about fifteen feet away bleeding out.

Blake realized how he could sell this as an accident. Thornton had been attacked by a wild boar. He had radioed Blake for help. When Blake arrived, Thornton tried to toss Blake the gun and accidentally shot himself. Blake grabbed the gun and shot the hog. He then tried to help Thornton, but it was too late.

You brought me out here to kill me, Blake said.

What? No. Why would I? Thornton asked.

What'd you want to talk to me about?

It took a moment before Thornton could speak. He wouldn't last much longer. I want to start an outdoors magazine, he said, his voice cracking, tears streaming from his eyes. I wanted to show you how beautiful it is out here, how fun. I figured if we bagged a big buck you'd be sold.

On what?

Writing for the magazine, he said, between quick, airy breaths. You're the only writer I know. I thought we could be partners.

Blake pulled back from Thornton. Really?

Yeah.

He could tell the man had only moments. There was blood everywhere. His face had lost all its color. His breathing was shallow and erratic.

I'm sorry, Thorn, he said. I'm so sorry.

Don't leave me.

I won't.

Would you have?

Left you?

Written for my magazine? he said.

Yeah, of course, man, Blake said. I'd be honored.

Really?

Really, Blake said. Why so surprised?

Brooke didn't think you would. Said not to even mention it to you until we'd been out here long enough for you to fall in love with the outdoors and hunting.

Brooke knew—

It was her idea to ask you, he said. Oh God, tell her I love her. And Zach. Tell him daddy . . .

Was a decent man who didn't deserve to die, Blake thought. That his mom killed him, and I was the weapon she used.

Barely Legal

From the moment young Becky Bonner arrived in Desperation to spend the summer with her Aunt Camille, everyone who knew Ronald McNair, or thought they did, knew it meant trouble.

By *trouble*, they imagined an attempted seduction or, at least, sexual harassment, but not what actually happened.

Though almost eighteen, Becky looked much younger. She was thin, with no discernable breasts, and her face, with its child-like features and big brown eyes had an innocent, little girl quality. She was almost of age, but without makeup, which she didn't wear, she looked way underage—just the way Ronald liked them.

President of Desperation Savings and Loan, Ronald McNair had money, position, and power—an unholy trinity that had allowed him to maintain an essentially pederast lifestyle unscathed. Of course, that was just town talk. Ronald had never been caught doing anything. None of the little part-timers and interns from the local high school and community college branch campus that he liked to employ had ever turned up pregnant or decried sexual harassment. But they were all of a certain type—very much like Becky—and they did get almost all of his time, attention, and affection.

It'd be sad and pathetic if it weren't so deviant and disgusting, a middle-aged man, a body betraying him—hair receding, lines marking the passage of time across a tired face, and a general all-around softening—obsessed with young girls less than half his age. This was how the citizens of Desperation thought about Ronald McNair, the ones who bothered to think about such things. The truth was, Ronald McNair was a reasonably attractive for his age in decent shape, and it was only in relation to young girls that he seemed sad or pathetic, disgusting or deviant.

No one was more aware of Ronald's predilection for PYTs than Becky's Aunt Camille, the longtime Desperation S&L branch manager. She and Ronald had worked together for over two decades, she doing the actual work, he the socializing and intern hiring. They had even had a thing some years back after Ronald's divorce, but she had been replaced by interns half her age, and neither of them spoke about it. Still, employees and patrons of the bank noticed how hard Camille worked at staying young looking—the narrow, emaciated frame, the too-young hair styles, the teenage fashions, the unvarnished face, and the ever (and mysteriously) decreasing breasts.

Given all this, people were shocked when Camille got Becky an interview with Ronald for one of his coveted summer internships. Their best guess, the ones voiced by those invested enough to venture one, was that Becky would be Camille's surrogate, pimped out by her own aunt just so she could get back in Ronald's personal life.

I'm not wearing any panties.

His eyes dropped down immediately to her short, straight skirt. When he looked up again, she was smiling. Maybe it was a smile. He wasn't sure. She was biting her lip a bit, but the corners of her mouth were definitely turned up.

God, he thought, how much that one little expression contained. Coyness. Innocence. Embarrassment. Flirtation. Challenge. Was there also invitation?

Oh really?

It's why I can't sit down, she said.

She was standing across from his enormous mahogany desk, him having just invited her in and offered her a seat.

She had a pretty, but plain face with eyes the color and shape of almonds, a narrow nose, and average-sized red lips, which looked slightly smallish when compared to the overly full, bee-stung protuberances that passed for lips these days. Her navy two-piece, single-breasted suit was professional enough, except for the too-short skirt, but she looked like a little girl playing dress up.

Do you usually go around without any panties?

No, sir. Not often. I had two suitcases.

You had two suitcases?

The airline lost one of them. The one with all my panties. I flew in late last night.

There's a certain amount of professionalism called for in banking, he said. Underwear isn't optional.

I started to ask Aunt Camille to reschedule the interview, but she's always talking about how cool you are, so I thought, fuck it. He'll understand.

And I do, he said. Airlines lose luggage.

Exactly.

Is he flirting with me? she wonders. Aunt Camille's right about him.

He nodded his understanding and looked down at her hot little body again. He couldn't help himself.

Take a picture, it lasts longer, she thought, the voice juvenile, obnoxious.

I'd really like the job, she said. And I promise to wear panties—unless you'd rather me not.

He wondered if she really had no panties (where were the ones she wore on the plane), or if she thought this little stunt would ensure her the internship. Or perhaps this was some twisted game her aunt had her playing. She was convinced (and had convinced quite a few other people) that he was obsessed with interns, but she was the obsessed one. Her jealousy had cost them their relationship.

Is she flirting with me? he wondered.

He didn't have the body of a twenty-year-old, but, for a man in his late forties, he hadn't completely let himself go. Of course, she could be turned on by money and power—two aphrodisiacs he had the appearance of having.

I have a lot of respect for Camille, he said. We're not just coworkers—

I know.

—but old friends. What does that mean?

I just know how close you two are. Or were.

Pausing a moment before continuing, he considered her. Well, I was just going to say that there's no way I could not give a relative of hers an opportunity. But that's all it is. An opportunity. Show me you can work hard and be professional. Don't embarrass me or your aunt. And get some underwear.

Thank you, Mr. McNair. Thank you so much.

Ronald, please.

Thank you, Ronald.

She said his name like a child with a new dirty word, stretching it out, lingering over the sounds, smiling at the way it tasted in her mouth.

You're welcome. Now go and tell your aunt that you two are coworkers.

He watched as she turned and began to bounce out of the office, a little voice inside his head whispering to him that he had just made a mistake. A mammoth one.

His eyes widened, as she reached the door, spotted something on the floor, and bent over to pick it up, her skirt rising as she did to reveal a small, tight, round, tanned bottom. At this, the whisper became a scream.

Whoops, she said, as she turned around and handed him the pen she had found on the floor. I forgot I wasn't . . .

Like hell you did, he thought, and knew he was in for the longest, hottest summer of his life.

Becky left Ronald's office feeling nauseated.

Why'd I agree to do this?

You'd do anything for Camille—like your mom says. Besides, it's for a good cause.

But he's so gross. Flirting with him gives me the creeps.

Is that it? Or is it that you're so good at it?

Like her mom and Camille, Becky had grown up without a father. What she knew of men and how to interact with them, she'd learned from TV magazines.

Being good at it is nothing special. Men are easy.

How'd it go? Camille asked.

Becky had just stepped into her private office in the back of the bank, which unlike Ronald's plush, pristine one in the front, was covered with stacks of papers and bank binders and printouts and disks and the incontrovertible evidence that actual work took place here.

I got the job.

Not what I asked.

It made me feel sick. It's just so—

Again, not what I asked.

I'm pretty sure I'll be playing the lead role in his fantasies for the foreseeable future.

Good girl. Just be careful.

That night, Ronald McNair, alone in his huge house, like nearly every night, undressed, removed his personal lubrication from the drawer beside his bed, fired up his laptop, and went in search of a certain type of women.

It was interesting. He liked variety—liked being with a different woman every night, but all the different women were strikingly similar.

But this night was different.

Instead of searching for women who looked like Camille—similar features, the same, shaved, narrow, tight bodies—he went to other sites.

Tonight, he roamed the teen sites, looking for Becky. She wasn't hard to find. In rows and rows of pictures of girls who looked way too young, way too juvenile to be on vetted sites, he found Becky after Becky—pubescents with no pubic hair and barely any breasts, innocent-faced schoolgirls of the Gone Wild, up-for-anything variety.

He was so aroused, he felt lightheaded. He honestly couldn't remember that last time he was this turned on.

Entering the fantasy, his surroundings and computer and his own actions fading, he made his bad girl intern his own.

The next morning, Becky's first day, Ronald was sitting at his desk reading the paper when she walked into his office and closed the door behind her.

He sat up. What is it?

My other suitcase came.

Good, he said slowly, the word sounding as much like a question as a statement.

I'm wearing panties, she said. See.

Lifting her short plaid skirt, she revealed a very small white cotton g-string thong, the tiny fabric of which barely covered what it was meant to in the front, while the thin thread, for it was little more than that, in the back accentuated the taut, shapely cheek on either side.

Ronald, pulse pounding, sweat beads popping, guiltily remembering his online activities from the night before, cleared his aroused-hoarse throat and said, I'm glad your things arrived, but you don't have to show me your underwear. I'll just trust that they're there.

Okay, but now you won't just have to use your imagination. You can picture them in your mind.

If Camille Clarkson had a religion it was exercise. Daily, she knelt at the alter of stretches and lunges, offering the sacrifice of her body to the gods of fitness and youth.

Every afternoon, at five minutes after five, she walked into the girls' restroom of the bank in a business suit and walked out in black capri running tights, a bright purple gym gilet with a hood in case it rained, and New Balance 755 running shoes with purple highlights to match her top.

At three minutes after five on this particular day, Candice Miller, a soft, round, middle-aged teller going to fat, tapped on the restroom door and walked in, not waiting for Camille to invite her.

Like the rest of the bank, the ladies' room was plush. Recently remodeled under Camille's supervision, the bright, clean, floral-smelling space was all marble counter tops, Italian tile, and brass fixtures.

Candice was slow and a little dull, and Camille had never liked her. She was the typical Desperation wife and mother, sinfully boring, living her sad little life for her spoiled, chubby kids and her fat, ignorant husband—an hourly-wage earner for the local electrical cooperative.

Hey, Camille, Candice said, admiring Camille's taut body. Can I talk to—Wow. You look amazing.

Thanks, Camille said.

She was out of her bank suit, but not yet in her workout clothes, and stood there in her bra and panties, lean, muscular, tan, a better body than women half her age.

You really do. I mean, you can't tell from your clothes just how spectacular your body really is.

I appreciate that, Candice, Camille said. What can I do for you?

I wanted to ask you a couple of things.

Camille waited, but Candice didn't continue. Okay.

I changed my mind about it. I was going to ask if I could work out with you. I need to lose a few pounds, but I can see you're way too advanced for me.

What'd you expect, you fat cow, Camille thought. I work my ass off while you fill yours with creme-filled cookies and snack cakes. A *few* pounds. Please.

Okay, so the other thing.

Do you do all this for Ronald? Candice asked. I mean, Mr. McNair. Are you two still . . . I mean are you—

Everything I do, I do for me, Camille said. I couldn't live with myself if I were fat and disgusting.

I know. I'm sorry. I didn't mean to . . . I just meant— Can I tell you something?

Could I stop you?

You're like my hero. You really are. You're so strong and independent. It's like you don't need anybody. I only asked about Mr. McNair because I care about you. I'm interested in you. I want to see you happy. I see all these young girls around here dressed like hookers, and you look better than all of them put together. You know? Anyway, I'm sorry. I shouldn't've said anything. Anyway, my second question was—

That wasn't it?

No, ma'am. That was just . . . me being stupid. My second one is . . . My back is bothering me.

Losing some weight will really help with that.

Ah, yeah. Well, I'm going to, but I wanted to talk to you about your breasts.

My—

Yeah. In the time I've known you they've gotten smaller. More to Ron—Mr. McNair's . . . Well, anyway I'd like to make mine smaller, and I wondered how you did it. Is there a certain exercise?

When you lose weight, your breasts get smaller, but not significantly. I mean, you can't exercise them away.

Are there hormones or drugs you can take?

Camille shook her head. The only real way is surgery.

Is that what you did?

No. I've never had surgery.

Then how'd you lose so much—

Camille unsnapped her bra and let it fall to the floor, the tile tinking as the metal snaps tapped it.

Oh my God, Candice said. You still have lots of . . . I mean, you're still so big, but I thought—

It's a minimizing bra, she said, bending to pick it up off the large square tile. This one's made by Lillyette. They're my favorite. They just make you look like you're small. It won't help you with your back.

So you just, I mean, you're just . . . for—

Ronald. Yes, Camille said. She wasn't sure exactly why she said it—the anger she felt at this tedious woman, her pent-up passion, the way Ron was frustrating her plan—but it felt good so she said more. It's why I shave and stay so small and don't wear makeup. It's all for a fucking man. I'm as pathetic as the rest of you. Now, if you'll excuse me, I really need to start my run.

As Camille ran, her words to Candice taunted her. How could she have been so impulsive? She'd never said anything like that out loud before—never even admitted it to herself. Not really.

How had Candice gotten her to make such a pathetic and embarrassing confession?

It had nothing to do with Candice and you know it.

Running through the depressed, dark, lifeless little town of Desperation, the stench of rotten egg pouring from the mill smoke that diffused the light of the sun and cast a gray haze over everything, she thought about the paltry existence of its inhabitants. Their small-minded, meager survival would not be her lot. She was meant for more. Destined for great things—but Ronald had been holding her back.

He had mocked her, made a mockery of what they had long enough. How could she have tolerated it so long? Could she be any more a victim, any more the embodiment of everything she hated? How the mighty are fallen. She had been brought low by a man—a man!

Well, no more. No longer. Soon, with Becky's help, he would be the one brought low. She was going to expose him for the demented prick he was.

Pushing herself, exercising every muscle she could, she was completely consumed with her desire for revenge. Though in pain, she smiled as she realized it wouldn't be long before she would exorcize Ronald McNair from her heart forever.

Ronald made a move on you yet? Camille asked.

Becky shook her head.

She was standing at the bathroom counter, looking into the mirror, straightening her hair. Camille was getting out of the shower behind her. Both women were nude.

Having never married nor having had any children of her own, Camille had always been more like a cool big sister to

Becky than an aunt, and sharing a bathroom, being completely naked around one another, was something they had always done.

I thought he would have by now, Becky said. He's always violating me with his eyes, but he's never done more than flirt—and he hasn't done much of that.

He will. Give him time.

As Camille finished drying off and stepped up to the mirror to brush her teeth, Becky noticed how alike they looked.

Her body's as good as mine, she thought. Maybe better.

They were essentially the same size, though Camille was more muscular. She's got bigger breasts, Becky thought, but I have nicer nipples. The only other difference was their pubic hair. Becky had it. Camille didn't.

Why do you shave your ah, hoo ha?

Habit, I guess, Camille said.

Did you do it for him?

Camille nodded. It drove him crazy. He said it was because it was easier to get to, but I think it made it easier for him to pretend.

Hearing Camille talk like this, Becky recalled her mom's warning that Camille had always been unstable, even a little unhinged. This was an odd conversation for a niece to be having with an aunt who was over twenty years her senior. In fact, the whole situation was odd, but her whole family was odd, always had been—and that included her mom. Yet what she had thought of as her mom's jealousy might actually have been a valid warning. Still, putting away a pervert was a good thing. She could get that done, then take off. But where could she go? She'd like to stay away from her mom's place until school started.

Camille looked up suddenly, excited, something had occurred to her. I know why he hasn't made his move yet. He's waiting for you to turn eighteen. We'll throw a big party. I bet you anything he'll make his move then.

I'm not wearing panties again, Becky said after walking into Ronald's office and closing the door.

I think we need to—

Because I shaved.

You *what?*

My first day without . . . you know, and I forget to wear panties.

Dropping onto the loveseat against the wall next to his desk, her short skirt rising on her thighs, Becky spread her legs.

Becky, you've really got to stop all this. I've tried not to say anything to Camille. I wouldn't want to embarrass her or create an awkward work environment, but this is going way too far.

I'll be eighteen tomorrow. Can I do it then?

You're a very attractive young woman, and I'm flattered, but this is inappropriate, and if you continue I'll have to tell your aunt to find you a different job.

I don't understand. I thought you liked—

I'm serious, Becky. I know what your aunt thinks—it ended our relationship—but she's wrong. I would never have a sexual relationship with a young girl.

Jumping up from his desk, Ronald stepped over to the door, opened it, and called for Camille. By the time she came into the office, Becky was standing, her skirt pulled down lower than it had been when she first arrived.

I was trying to avoid doing this, Ronald said to Camille, but it just isn't possible. You've got Becky believing the same crazy things you do about me and interns. She's making inappropriate suggestions and advances, and it's got to stop. I think it's best if you find Becky a different job this summer. We'll still have the party for her tomorrow night, but after that . . . she just needs to works somewhere else.

Becky, would you excuse us a minute? Camille asked.

Becky, looking innocent and confused, left the room.

I apologize if anything I said caused Becky to act out some sort of sexual fantasy. She's a troubled young woman, and I should have been more careful. I called myself protecting her, warning her. I had no idea she would—

I can't believe you think you have to warn her about me. How can you still believe that?

If I'm wrong, I'm sorry, Camille said, but I've been around here a long time. I see who you hire and how you act around them.

It's just your perception, your jealousy. You've turned your wild speculation into an obsession.

Don't forget who you're talking to. I know what you like. Your dirty little secrets.

He remembered the time, when they were still together, she borrowed his laptop and stumbled upon some of the sites he frequented. That was when all this began. When she saw his screen fill with graphic images intended to elicit a response—just not the response she had. Arousal, not revulsion, was their purpose, but she was incapable of separating fantasy from reality, and that was when her crusade began.

Fantasies. You know *some* of my fantasies. That's all they are. And if you weren't so damned uptight and controlling you might have some yourself. I thought we could work together, but now I'm not so sure.

She started to say something, but stopped, took in a deep breath, and let it out very slowly.

I'm sorry. You're right. I just got a little overwrought.

It keeps happening and I keep allowing it. I've been—

We can work together.

I don't think we can.

I'll show you. I promise. You'll see.

You're nearly irreplaceable, which is why I haven't done anything sooner. Nearly, but not completely. No one is.

I'll do better. I see now. I really do. Give me one more chance. If it happens again, I'll resign. I promise.

This is the last chance. The very last.

Thank you. You won't be sorry. I'm gonna—

Let's put all this behind us. We'll throw Becky a great eighteenth birthday party, find her a different job, and see if you and I can move forward.

Becky wished there were someone she could call, an adult, preferably male, she could trust, who'd tell her the truth, who'd give her some perspective, but there was no one. She was beginning to doubt both Ronald's guilt and Camille's sanity.

As her concerns had intensified, she had spent some time researching sexual fantasy, and discovered just how common and healthy they were—among men and women. It seemed everyone was fantasizing except her aunt.

She had thought about her own fantasies—the way she wanted to be taken forcibly, told what to do, ravished by a group of guys, have sex with a woman, do it in a public place, be watched, and even have sex with a much older man. God, if Camille knew any of this.

According to the experts, very few people ever acted out their fantasies. Was Ronald among the few who did? Camille was convinced he was, but Becky wasn't so sure anymore.

She couldn't ask her mom. She was as crazy as Camille.

She ran the list of male teachers she'd had and the fathers of her friends—the few that had them—but there was no one.

You're on your own, kiddo.

He's just not taking the bait, Becky said.

She and Camille were in front of the bathroom mirror again, this time fully clothed in brand-new dresses they'd gotten for the party, solid sheer shifts with colorful beaded fronts, Camille's purple, Becky's lavender. In their coordinating outfits, they looked far more like sisters than aunt and niece.

He will.

I'm not so sure. Maybe it really is just fantasy.

That's how it starts with all of them.

Why do some cross the line into reality and some don't?

All do eventually.

Why do grown men like teenage girls anyway?

Youth. Beauty. Innocence. Tightness. Thinness. They were once teenagers themselves and could have had teenage girls, but they were too awkward and inexperienced, so they want a do-over. Remember, they're still just teenage boys inside.

I don't know. Maybe it's me.

You're perfect. It's not you. It's him. He's crafty. He's been doing this a long time without getting caught.

I've done everything I know to do.

Let's give it just a little longer. At least until after the party.

When Camille had called, Becky had been only too happy to help her favorite aunt catch a predator, but the task was proving to be far more difficult than she had imagined, and she was beginning to think he might not be guilty after all. Maybe he was right. Maybe Camille was just jealous, obsessive, and a little unstable.

Okay, Becky said. But if he doesn't do something soon, I'd like to stop. I've done about all of this I can stomach.

Becky's eighteenth birthday party took place in the back of the bank in the executive suite comprised of the boardroom, the kitchen, and the recently remodeled employee lounge.

All the bank employees and most of their significant others were there. They had come for two primary reasons (since they hadn't known Becky long and really didn't know her well). None of them passed up an opportunity to party, and they were all loyal to Camille, fully aware that it was her competence that gave them job security and increased the value of their stock.

Everyone was in attendance except for Ronald McNair.

Slipping out of the boardroom with two glasses of the driest white wine she could find, Camille walked through the dark, quiet bank to Ronald's office in the front.

His door was closed, but the slight hint of illumination peeked out from beneath. She knew from previous nocturnal assignations what it meant. Only his desk lamp was on.

Two quick, quiet taps, and she was inside.

I got you something, she said, handing him the wine.

Taking the wine, he said, Thanks.

You're welcome, but that's not it. I wanted to say I'm sorry for . . . well, for losing my mind. I know my jealousy messed up what we had and I'm sorry.

Thank you, he said, his voice rich with surprise and appreciation. That *is* better than the wine.

You're welcome, but that's not it either.

What I got you, what I'm about to give you, is the best blow job of your life.

Kicking the chair back, she knelt down before him, quickly unzipping and pulling down his pants, clutching him with her hand, taking him into her mouth.

She knew what he liked and it didn't take long.

When she could speak again, she said, Do you accept my apology?

Back at the party, Camille made a concerted effort to mingle. She had missed the opening of the presents, but no one seemed to notice how long she'd been gone. Out of boredom, she drank more than she normally did and then began looking for Becky.

Camille asked around, but no one seemed to know where she was. Then she ran into Candice Miller.

Have you seen Becky?

She looked around the room, jerking her head about. Ronald called her to his office to give her his present, but she should've been back by now. That was—

Come on, Camille said.

The two women walked through the dark lobby, Camille in front, her steps angry, aggressive. Candice couldn't keep up.

Without slowing or knocking, Camille flung the door open.

Immediately, she began to yell as she charged McNair, knocking him out of his chair, jumping on him and pounding his face with the bottoms of her fists.

With Camille no longer blocking her view, Candice could see what had propelled her to the violence that still gripped her. There, splayed out across his desk was the completely naked and unconscious body of her niece.

Snatching up the phone just inches from Becky's small, pale left breast, Candice called the police.

I'm so sorry, Camille said.

You've gotta stop saying that.

It was a week later. The two women were seated in the office of the lead investigator of the Desperation Police Department.

I'm okay, Becky said. I promise.

If I had known ... Camille began. I should have known. What was I thinking?

That we'd get a pedophile off the street and we did.

So, according to your statement, Detective Harry Lanier said, you suspected Mr. McNair of inappropriate relationships with young girls and were setting him up.

Originally, but we both came to believe that he was innocent, Camille said. I even talked to him about us getting back together. I just can't believe I was so stupid. And I'm so sorry Becky had to go through this. It was never my intention for anything to happen to—

I don't want to talk about it, Becky said. Hell, I don't even want to think about it.

We thought we had been wrong about him, but he was waiting for her to turn eighteen.

But she didn't, right? Lanier asked. It wasn't her real birthday.

Right. She doesn't turn eighteen until September, Camille said.

Do you have enough to convict him? Becky asked.

More than enough, Lanier said. Don't you worry. Between the GHB in your system and his semen on your dress—

Do I have to be in here for this? Becky asked.

No, Camille said without waiting for a response from Lanier. You go on home and finish packing. I'll finish up and meet you back at the house.

When Becky was gone, Camille said, You've got his semen on her dress. What else?

Really, that's about it, but it's enough.

I don't want her subjected to a trial. Has he been offered a plea?

Lanier nodded. He hasn't taken it yet—says he can't remember anything. I don't know. I just wish I knew what he had been up to.

Whatta you mean?

It's nothing. Every case has them. Little things that you can never quite get to fit.

Such as?

It's nothing. Really.

I want to know.

It's just . . . she was naked when you and Candice got there, right?

Camille nodded.

That's just strange. Why, ah, ejaculate on her dress just to take it off? In my experience, once a guy like this, ah, shoots his load, pardon my French, he's not good for much else. Why do it, then take her dress off and lie her on the desk?

What does he say?

Says he doesn't remember any of it. Swears he didn't do anything.

Isn't that what they all say?

He was unconscious when we arrived.

Because his head hit the floor, and then I pounded his face with my fists. I want to see him.

When Becky was alone, her mind wandered, but always wound up back at the same place. What had he done to her? Where had he touched her? What was the extent of his violations?

As she packed her things, anxious to be as far away from Ronald and Camille and the bank and Desperation as possible, she wondered if not knowing exactly what had happened to her was better or if her imagination was making the experience far more traumatic than it had actually been.

She was pondering this when she stepped into Camille's large walk-in closet to look for the spaghetti strap floral print drawstring blouse she had let her borrow and found instead her lavender shift. It was on the floor beneath the hanging dresses, behind the laundry basket.

At first, she was confused. How did it get here? Shouldn't it be in the DPD evidence room?

When she picked it up and examined it and saw there were no semen stains on it, everything began to fall into place. She remembered Camille giving her a drink and telling her Ronald wanted to see her, and not much after that—except opening her eyes briefly as she was being loaded into the ambulance and seeing her Aunt Camille wearing her lavender shift. She switched dresses with me, she thought. She drugged my drink and switched dresses with me and set Ronald up. Mom was right. She's the sick one, not him. Oh my God. What a twisted, demented . . . Why didn't I see it sooner?

Sitting alone in the small, dank, cage-like jail cell had given Ronald McNair a lot of time for reflection. He pondered many things, the quality of his life, the good he had done, the damage. On balance, he felt like he had lived a decent life. He could have done more. He regretted not giving more of his money to good causes, but pledged to do more when all this was behind him.

What he couldn't get past, what continued to torment his thoughts, was what exactly he had done. He had fantasies, sure, but he had never acted on them. Had they led him here. Did he finally snap and act out on one of his infatuations?

If people knew the things he had done in his mind . . . But that wasn't the same, was it? That doesn't lead to drugging and raping teenage girls, does it?

Why did he go to all those teen porn sites? What was wrong with him? Ever since Becky Boner had shown him what was hidden beneath her skirt, he had been fucking her in his mind, returning time and again to the online portals featuring girls who looked like her. Since then, he hadn't been able to quit feeding the insatiable, horny teenage Ron that lived inside him.

Camille, I swear to you I didn't touch her, Ronald was saying.

But Mr. President, the evidence is all over her dress.

They were in the visitation room at the jail, seated in folding chairs, a folding table between them. Ronald had shuffled in a few minutes before in handcuffs and shackles to find Camille chatting familiarly with the big, pale inmate orderly.

I don't know what happened, but I do know what I'm not capable of. The certitude and conviction of this statement was undermined by the guilty memory of his fantasies.

Camille didn't say anything.

Do you know Remington? he asked.

What? Why do you ask?

You two seemed very friendly when I walked in.

How many have there been?

How many what?

Interns. Underage girls. How many?

I've never touched a single one. Not one. You saw how aggressive your niece was. All I did was discourage her. Redirect her. And if it weren't for you, I would've fired her.

Me?

Don't be daft, Camille. You know I love you. Always have.

I'd find it easier to believe if you hadn't raped my seventeen-year-old niece.

I didn't. I keep telling you. And she's eighteen.

Actually, she's not.

I was at her party.

That was just a ruse to see if you'd try anything with her. I never dreamed you'd rape her.

I didn't. Whatta you mean ruse?

They were alone in the large, open room, except for a deputy in the corner keeping an eye on them and Remington, who was near the opposite wall, mopping the already sparkling floor. Ronald couldn't believe he was actually in jail.

You've been fooling around with these young girls for years, but I could never catch you.

Because I haven't been.

You must think I'm the most—

You set me up? he asked. You used your own niece for bait and you—but I didn't take the bait. I never touched her. Hardly even looked at her, so what . . . you . . . Suddenly, the light of revelation registered in his eyes. So you seduced me.

You had me fooled into believing that you were actually innocent. I thought we might be together again.

Ronald sat silent for a moment, gazing up as everything began to fall into place.

You sick bitch. You came into my office and sat on my desk and spread your legs and gave me head . . . and what? Let me come in your mouth, so you could put it on Becky's dress. Did you drug the glass of wine you brought me? Drug poor Becky? I didn't do what you thought I would—because I'm not a pedophile, have never touched a young girl—so, because you're so sick and twisted and jealous and see all kinds of wickedness where there isn't any, you took matters into your own hands—and mouth, he added with a hard laugh—and framed me. You sick . . . You—you'll never get away with it.

I already have, she said standing.

I know now. I'll get out. You just wait. I meet with my attorney in the morning and—

Leaning over and putting her lips next to his ear, she whispered, You won't make it 'til morning. You're a child molester. You'll get shanked. Well, raped and then shanked.

She jerked her head over toward Remington, and he turned to look at him. The large, neo-Nazi looking man was staring back with equal parts menace and pleasure.

I'm about to die, Ronald thought. I'm gonna die and there's nothing I can do about it. Why, God? Why is this happening to me? Am I being punished? For what? Lust?

Fantasizing about a young girl? I don't deserve this. It's not fair. It's not right. I'm a good man.

Camille turned and began walking away.

Ronald jumped up, reaching for her.

Please, Camille. Please, no. Oh God. I didn't do anything. I swear I never did anything to any of them. I—

He broke off suddenly when she turned toward him, and he caught a glimpse of something behind her eyes. She was insane. Reasoning with her was as futile as anything else he could do right now.

Sit down, inmate, the deputy yelled, standing to meet Camille. I'm walking her out. Sit still until I get back.

Don't leave me alone with—

Shut the fuck up, pedophile. Turning to Remington, he said, Hey Remy, keep an eye on this prick 'til I get back.

Sure thing, boss, Remington said, putting down his mop and walking toward Ronald with a wolfish smile on his face. Be happy to.

Making Amends

The only Alcoholics Anonymous meeting in Desperation, Florida, meets in the small, dim, musty smelling fellowship hall of the Episcopal Church on Monday and Thursday evenings. Like most AA meetings around the world, the smells permeating the room are coffee and cigarette smoke—for though members can't smoke inside the church building, the stale, acrid aroma wafts in with them, emanates off their clothes, and spews out of their mouths.

Each meeting begins the same way—with a staple of AA gatherings everywhere, the Serenity Prayer.

In unison, the men and women known only by their first names inside the meeting (outside, in the small town, everyone knows everything about everybody) say, God grant me the serenity to accept the things I cannot change; courage to change the things I can; and wisdom to know the difference.

The group consists of regulars, occasionals, and strangers. The regulars are a handful of people—a waitress from the diner, the Episcopal priest, a retired judge, a homemaker/full-time mom, an electrical contractor, and a middle-aged mill worker—who are committed to their recovery and rarely miss. The occasionals are a rotating group of mostly men who are court ordered to attend because of DUIs. The strangers, of which there are seldom any, are drop-ins, mostly people in town for work or to visit family or, ever so often, someone who drives over from a nearby town in an attempt to keep the fact that they're an alcoholic truly anonymous.

The biweekly assemblings mostly alternate between Step and Speaker meetings, and on this Monday evening in January, the topic is Step Eight: Made a list of all persons we had harmed, and became willing to make amends to them all.

Hi, my name is Maria and I'm an addict, the striking blonde waitress with the big brown eyes says.

Hi, Maria, the group says in unison.

I've got to tell you, of all the steps this one is the most difficult for me—well, this one and the next one. For some very complicated reasons I am unable to make amends to the people I've harmed the most.

Most everyone nods, but no one is more understanding or shows more empathy than the elderly Episcopal priest. Beneath a smattering of white hairs on a mostly bald head, Harry's big blue eyes are some of the kindest she's ever seen.

Hi, my name is Craig and I'm an alcoholic, the tall, electrical contractor with the large hands says.

Hi, Craig.

I didn't have nearly as much trouble with this step or the next one as I did four and five, he says. It took me forever to admit to myself the exact nature of my addiction and what it has caused me to do, but once I finally got honest with myself, everybody else has been a snap.

As the discussion of Step Eight continues, Maria's attention becomes increasingly focused on the only stranger in attendance. When given the opportunity to introduce himself at the beginning of the meeting he refrained, and, now halfway through the discussion, he has yet to utter a word.

She finds herself drawn to him, and has to be careful not to stare. Experiencing sexual stirrings inside like she hasn't in a very long time, she's even more moved with compassion.

In the past several years, Maria has become an expert on people. She has studied so many for so long, she can read nearly anyone, and now the full weight of her perceptive eye is trained on the stranger.

He's quite handsome, with straight light brown hair and deep, dark, sad brown eyes, not unlike her own. He's tall and lean, with a good face. He's confident, and he's hiding something.

Like me, she thinks, he has a secret.

Buy you a cup of coffee? Maria asks.

The stranger hesitates, but just a moment, then says, Sure.

He had lingered after the meeting, observing, eavesdropping, and when he finally left, Maria had followed him out into the small grass parking lot on the side of the fellowship hall.

I'm Maria, she says.

Hi, Maria, he says, mocking the sing-song greeting from the meeting.

And you are? she asks.

Eddie, he says.

Come on, Eddie, she says. I'll introduce you to the best key lime pie in the state.

So what's your story? Maria asks.

I hear you're the one with the interesting story, he says. Or lack there of. You're the closest thing to a mystery they've got around here.

His words remind her how careless she's being. For five years, she's lived in solitude, avoided social situations, personal interactions outside of work, and intimacy of any kind. Now, she's actually on a date with a stranger.

Be careful, she tells herself. Make sure you know what you're doing.

I'm an outsider, she says. Even after five years. Didn't grow up here. Don't have any family. Haven't shared much of my back story.

Much? he says, his voice rising.

Any, she says.

They're seated in a booth in the Desperation Diner on Main Street in downtown. The Monday night crowd is virtually nonexistent—especially after the dinner hour, which is how Maria's able to get Mondays off. Typically small town, the diner is in desperate need of repair and remodeling—something Maria is more acutely aware of seeing it through Eddie's eyes.

You work here? he asks.

She nods.

It feels funny to be sitting in a booth like any other customer. She never dates, and on the few occasions she eats out, it isn't here where she knows the kitchen and the cooks so intimately.

Sandy, their waitress, a large, blonde girl with fair skin and pale blue eyes, arrives and when Eddie isn't looking, she raises her eyebrows to Maria.

Two cups of coffee, Eddie says, and a couple of slices of whatever's on the third shelf of that thing, he adds, jerking his head toward the glass desert case and its spinning carrousel of pies.

Two cups of coffee and two slices of key lime coming up, she says, and walks away, a hint of irritation drifting off her like cheap, pungent perfume.

She mad about something? Eddie asks.

Small order, she says. Little tip.

Not necessarily.

They're quiet a moment, and Maria is able to study Eddie some more—this time from much closer and with better light. What she sees confirms her earlier observations. He's good and kind, but wounded and hardened by some kind of trauma—probably a recent one. He still seems raw.

How'd you know about me? she asks. What're you doing here?

I'm looking for someone, he says.

That all I get?

You don't give anything, but you want me to?

Uh huh.

The only other booth occupied in the diner holds an atypical interracial couple—white man/black woman—who always eat late to avoid the small southern town crowd they make so uncomfortable.

I owe a guy some money, he says, and I'm trying to find him.

She actually laughs out loud. Does anyone ever buy that?

You'd be surprised how many gullible people there are in the world.

I'm surprised you think *I'm* one of them.

I don't, he says. I was just kidding. I don't want to get into the specifics, but I'm here looking for someone to . . . let's just say the step tonight is a sign I'm in the right place at the right time.

Here to make amends. To who? Or is it whom?

I'm not sure—I mean about the person, not the who or whom thing. It's whom.

How can you not—

It's complicated.

It always is.

I hurt someone very badly, he says, and by extension I hurt someone else. I'm looking for the someone else.

Boyfriend? she asks. Husband?

He smiles. Did you know that the word 'amend' comes from two Latin words that mean to X out fault.

He's obviously trying to direct the conversation off the specifics.

Our word 'amend' means to put right, he continues. Especially in the sense of a text, as in emendation?

No, but I should have, she says. Words are sort of my thing.

Then you'll appreciate this. To amend something is to make a modification for the better, to improve. It's not just to change, but change for good. That's why Step Nine says we should make direct amends to such people wherever possible, *except* when to do so would injure them or others.

Tuesday, Wednesday, and Thursday, Eddie spent interviewing more townspeople, asking questions of everyone—particularly those in the AA group. He was good at it, too, skillfully extracting information from distrusting people who didn't willingly part with it.

Nearly all his questions centered around New Year's Eve, and when Maria heard, she knew it involved the hit-and-run death of the late-teens/early-twenties Jane Doe on the curve near the Stump Hole.

Did you kill her? Maria asks.

Eddie doesn't say anything, but something about the way the light in his eyes changes makes her think he did.

They're standing in the grass field next to the Episcopal Church fellowship hall where she had been waiting for him to show up for the Thursday night meeting.

You did, didn't you? she says. You hit her and drove away like a coward.

If I did, am I beyond forgiveness, beyond help?

No, she says. You're not. We've all done things . . . we . . .

Our speaker's unable to be with us tonight, Father Harry Franklin says, so we're going to discuss step nine.

The group consists of the same people from Monday night with one exception. Joining the others is a thin, jittery young man with pale skin and unkempt black hair. His gaunt face is drawn, his hooded eyes, slivers of moons above the black-as-night circles beneath them. His presence seems to make everyone uncomfortable, but no one more so than Harry.

Made direct amends to such people wherever possible except when to do so would injure them or others, Harry is saying.

How do we know for sure? Eddie asks.

Hi, I'm Harry, and I'm an alcoholic, Father Franklin says. And you are?

Eddie, he says.

Welcome, Eddie, he says. How do we know what?

When making amends would actually injure someone.

It's a good question, Harry says. One that doesn't have a single answer. Each situation is different. Perhaps you'd like to share an example with the group and we can let you know what we think.

He knows, Maria thinks. They all do. They want to hear him say what he did. But why? To help him or to report him to the police?

Well, okay. As a hypothetical, what if you hurt someone very badly, but they didn't know it? They've already experienced the pain of what you've done. Does it help them to let them know you're the one who did it?

You be a little more specific? Kevin asks.

Not really.

We've all done things we don't want to own up to, but we need to for the sake of our sobriety.

An uncomfortable silence follows Kevin's words, and everyone stares at Eddie.

Do I make you guys nervous? Eddie asks.

Not at all, Harry says, but it comes out too fast and sounds insincere.

I know I've been asking a lot of questions around town, and a lot of people are talking about me, but I thought I'd find understanding here. Sympathy. I'm just hear to do what AA is all about. I want to make amends.

Obviously, we appreciate that, Harry says.

We just want you to be honest, Kevin says. I don't think you're leveling with us.

Wait now, Maria says. We're not here to evaluate each other, but to support.

She's right, Harry says. Thanks for reminding us, Maria.

We're not just here for support, but for accountability, Kevin says. I'm just saying we've got to be honest with ourselves.

You're right, Kevin, we do, Harry says, but only we can truly know when we are.

But if we think one of the group is lying, don't we have a responsibility to call him on it?

Harry's eyes narrow.

Kevin glares back. Challenging.

Yes, I guess we do.

But, Maria says, only out of love and genuine concern, only after we've built a relationship with the person and they can trust us.

Trust, Eddie says. That's interesting. Can we trust each other? I'm new to AA. How anonymous is it?

What do you mean? Harry asks.

Well, for instance, if someone in the group confesses to—I don't know, say, committing a crime, have you ever had anyone in the group report the person to the police?

We've got to be able to say anything in here, Maria says. This only works if we know this is a safe place.

She's right, Harry says. You can tell us anything.

Anything, Kevin says.

What was that between Father Franklin and Kevin last night?

He is seated in a booth by himself at almost closing time on Friday night. The diner is empty, and Maria lingers every time she brings something to his table, which is often.

Confessor's remorse? she asks. I don't know. I think some people confess to Harry and then later regret it. Be one thing if they didn't really interact with him, but to see him so often and so intimately in the meeting . . . I think it can lead to fear and even resentment.

Ever happen to you?

She nods.

Wonder what Kevin's hiding?

We're all hiding something, she says.

Some of us more than others.

She nods again, slower, more considered this time.

Did you mean what you said? he asks.

What?

I'm not beyond forgiveness.

Of course.

Can you forgive me?

It's not my place.

Can you get past it, I mean?

She stares at him for a long moment, then nods.

What time do you get off?

He wants to go home with me, she thinks. Don't let him. You've already done too much. Don't do that. Don't sleep with him.

You're my last customer, she says. Why?

You as lonely as you seem?

Her eyes glisten and she takes a step back.

I am too, he says. Let's do something together. We can go out. I can come home with you. We can talk or not. Whatever you're comfortable with.

They had both had better sex before—but it'd been so long that this average encounter makes them nearly euphoric.

As the shudders end and their pulses slow, the underlying sadness that seems so essential to them both returns.

Thought you said you were out of practice, he says.

He's on his back, upper body propped up on pillows. She's next to him, her head on his chest, her arm around him. Both naked, a thin white sheet is draped across their lower bodies. Like the room and the mobile home it's in, the bed is small and merely functional. There is nothing fancy in Maria's life. Instead of jewelry or perfume, her dresser holds books, most of which are about addiction recovery.

I used not to be half bad, she says.

You're great, he says. So beautiful. So generous.

You ever gonna tell me the whole truth of why you're here? Maria asks.

In your bed?

In Desperation.

Who do you think the victim was?

She doesn't have to ask which victim he means.

Wasn't local, she says. Was, someone would've known her.

Then what?

Hitchhiker, maybe. Runaway of some sort. Someone just passing through.

Or here to meet someone, he says.

Was she?

He nods.

So your questions are yielding results.

Some, he says. Not enough.

Eddie waits in the darkness, watching the small rectory window.

When the soft glow of the lamp comes on, Eddie steps out from behind the hedge at the side of the property and walks toward the back door near the priest's office.

Seated at his desk, lit from the small pool of light reflecting off the large blotter, Harry looks old and weary, small and feeble.

As Eddie steps from the hallway into the study, the old priest jerks his head up, eyes wide and frightened.

What's a man of the cloth got to be so jumpy about?

Huh?

Who're you expecting?

Sorry, Harry says, recovering quickly, plastering a pleasant expression on his face. You startled me. I thought I was alone.

You were. Now you're not.

How can I help you? Harry says.

Just dropped by to say hi.

Sure there's not something on your mind?

No, not really.

Well, okay.

Lot of people in town confess to you, don't they?

A few, he says. It's more talking than formal confessions.

Kevin seemed to—

Seemed to what? Kevin asks, as he appears in the open doorway.

Eddie turns to face him.

You okay, Harry? Kevin asks.

I'm fine, Harry says. Eddie and I are just having a little chat.

About me?

No.

Either of you know anything about the hit-and-run New Year's Eve? Eddie says.

Why do you ask? Kevin says.

I'm asking everybody.

Why?

Do you know who the victim is? Eddie asks.

Was.

Was, Eddie says. Or anything about her?

Lifting his eyebrows and staring pointedly at Eddie, Kevin shrugs and says, I might know something.

Such as.

Such as who did it, he says. Information the police might find interesting.

Kevin, Harry says. You're not threatening Eddie, are you?

No.

You know he's here to make amends.

I'm not threatening anyone, he says. Just saying we need to get to doing what it is we're here to do.

He saw you? Maria says.

Says he did.

They're beside his car outside the church. She had waited for him again, and now they're both late for the meeting.

You think he'll go to the police? Maria asks.

Eddie shrugs.

But clearly it was a threat.

Maybe, but more than anything else, it was a mistake. A very big one.

Hi, my name's Eddie and I'm an alcoholic.

Hi, Eddie, the group responds.

The young woman who was killed on New Year's Eve, he says. It was my fault, and I'm here to make amends. As Eddie's voice cracks and tears start to moisten his eyes, he stands and pulls out a picture. Her name was Hope. She was here to meet someone. If you saw her or know who she was with that night, please tell me so I can do what's right. Please.

Later that night, as Maria and Eddie are having coffee and pie in the diner, a detective from the sheriff's department pulls up outside.

So much for confidentiality, Eddie says.

You don't know he's here to—

Sure I do, he says. Someone in the group, let's call him Kevin, dropped a dime on me.

Talk to you a minute? the detective asks.

Without waiting for a response, he slides in next to Maria.

I'm Detective Morrell, he says. With the sheriff's department.

Have a seat, Eddie says. Want some pie?

Just information.

The detective is young, pale, and pudgy, his wet-looking hair parted on the side and combed over.

Sure, Eddie says. Anything for the cause of justice.

Where were you on New Year's Eve between the hours of ten and two?

Which year?

This past one.

Eddie seems to think about it. You know, I can't recall.

I thought you were gonna help the cause of justice.

Withholding information in a criminal investigation is a crime.

I've heard.

Okay, he says, sighing and frowning in frustration. Suit yourself. The hard way it is.

Things're heatin' up, Eddie says.

You seem to want them to, Maria says, but I can't imagine why.

They're lying in Maria's bed, he on his back, she on her stomach next to him, her arm draped over his chest. All the covers have long since been kicked off the bed, exposing their moist, naked bodies.

The only movement in the room comes from the slow revolutions of the wood and wicker blades on the ceiling fan above them.

Maria pushes herself up and looks at him. How does bringing things to a boil help you? Are you trying to make sure you get punished? Do you want to get caught?

He shakes his head.

Then what exactly?

He starts to say something, but stops.

Ready to exchange secrets? she asks. I'd like to know what you're really up to.

He doesn't say anything.

Here I go, she says. I'm going to tell you everything, and then you can decide if you want to trust me back.

When she's finished with her story*, Eddie realizes he can tell her anything and there's nothing she can do. Like him, she doesn't want to spend any more time with the cops than she has to.

Remember when I said Kevin made a mistake in what he said to me?

Yeah.

He couldn't have seen me, he says. I wasn't there.

But—

I didn't hit Hope, he says. I wasn't anywhere near Desperation that night.

But you told the group—

I haven't lied about anything. Hope was here because of me—because I encouraged her to be. She met this guy at FSU where she's working on a degree in psychology. I mean was. It was love at first sight—at least for her. She wasn't sure how he felt. They met at the end of the semester, right before the holidays, and the whole time she was home for Christmas, he was all she could think about. After talking to a few of his friends, she found out he would be at a New Year's Eve party at a beach house his parents have not far from here. I could tell she wanted to show up at the party and surprise him, but she's too shy, too reserved, too much like her mother to do anything like that, but I insisted.

Her mom? she says. You're married?

He shakes his head. She died several years ago. Hope was all I had. I not only gave her permission to miss my annual New Year's Eve bash, but forbid her to come.

Yours?

I own a company in Fort Walton Beach, he says. The party's for my friends and family as much as my employees. I told her that this grand romantic gesture would be something her children would tell her grandchildren about someday. And even if things didn't work out with this guy, she wanted to be the kind of person who did things like this. So to please her

* See *Death of a Desperate Woman*

dad as much as anything else, she came here looking for a boy whose name I don't even know, who none of her friends even know about—and not just because they just met, but because of how private she is. She is so secretive, so easily embarrassed. I pushed her into doing something she never would have done otherwise, and it got her killed.

Tears are rolling out of his eyes and filling his ears.

Oh God, Eddie, I'm so sorry.

He tries to say something, but breaks down and begins to sob.

You blame the boy? she asks. That why you're trying to find him?

He shakes his head. I found out this weekend who he is. He's back at FSU. Had nothing to do with her death. Didn't even know about it. She never made it. Her car broke down just outside of Panama City. A friend of hers was supposed to go with her, but backed out at the last second. I didn't know. I thought someone was with her. She called me several times, but the music at the party was so loud I never heard my phone. She left me the sweetest messages. When she couldn't get me, she didn't know what to do, then a nice elderly couple picked her up and gave her a ride to just outside of Desperation. She was trying to get another one when she was murdered.

They never found her car, she says.

It was stolen later that night.

And you never told the police? she asks. Never identified the body?

He shakes his head.

This whole time you've been here looking for . . .

The drunk fuck who ran over her and ran away.

You used me.

No.

The group. AA.

A little. Yeah.

You lied.

No. I just didn't tell you everything. But I am now.

You're going to . . .

Make amends, he says. Put things right. Change things for good.

This whole time I felt so sorry for you, she says. I moved past what I thought you had done. Let you in my heart, my bed.

Please try to understand, he says. I've got to do this. And what I feel for you is real. It has nothing to do with—

Killing the person who accidentally hit your daughter won't do that, she says.

Don't do that, he says. Don't call it an accident. Getting in the driver's seat drunk is no accident.

You don't know he was drunk.

The group wouldn't be so nervous if he wasn't, he says. Or if it isn't one of them.

Please don't do this, she says.

I have to.

You won't feel any better, she says. It won't bring her back.

I know.

Your life will be over, she says. They say when you seek revenge, dig two graves.

You think I care? Nothing matters to me—nothing—except ending the life of the man who ended the life of my precious little . . . She was so good, so kind, so sweet. Never caused me one minute's trouble—even after her mom died. She was pure joy. Never hurt anyone. I never heard her say an unkind or hurtful thing about another person. Not once.

Then you've got to know she wouldn't want you to do this.

You can't talk me out of this, he says.

They are quiet a moment.

So Kevin . . .

Was out there that night, he says. I've already confirmed that. And he couldn't have seen me.

You think he did it.

And confessed to Harry.

Why do you seem happy about that?

I've found out a lot about the good folks of this little town while I've been here, he says. Harry isn't in recovery as much as he pretends to be.

Tell me who it is, Eddie is saying.

Who *who* is? Harry asks.

You know what. Who's the hit-and-run driver. I know you know, and one way or another you're going to tell me.

They are in the priest's small bedroom where Eddie has awakened him with a hand over his mouth.

Even if I knew, I couldn't tell you, he says.

The room is dark except for the light beneath the bedside lamp. The aging priest looks washed out, overexposed by his proximity to the bulb, his loose, wrinkled skin and weak, tired eyes adding to the appearance of fragility.

I've learned quite a bit about you the past week or so, Eddie says. Never been married have you? Though not exactly celibate either.

I'm Episcopalian, not Catholic, he manages with a bit of what might be defiance.

True, Eddie says, and if you lived in another part of the country your sex life might not be much of an issue, but you live in the deep south. You know what they say about the south. What's worse? Being caught with a black woman or a white man?

The priest doesn't say anything, just looks away.

I'd say the man is worse, Eddie says. As racist as these backwoods are, they're more homophobic. Can't stand the idea of boys kissing, can they? And guess what I have pictures of?

Tears form in Harry's eyes.

You doing a lot more than kissing. You're an all-star. Pitcher *and* catcher. I'm having glossies made for your entire congregation. Eleven by seventeens for your bishop. You always drink a lot before, during, and after, don't you? I mean, *a lot*. And isn't Kevin a little young for you? Is he blackmailing you? Is that it? Can't go to the police because he'll expose you?

Please.

Now that's an interesting word. One that haunts me. I keep wondering if Hope said it as she died. 'Please, God.' 'Please, Daddy.' 'Please don't let me die.' 'Please make it stop hurting.' She was always so polite. Even in excruciating pain she would have said 'please.' Of course, she could've died instantly—never knew what hit her, or who. Isn't that funny? That's my only consolation, the best case scenario—that she was killed immediately. Wasn't lying, bones broken, bleeding to death in a ditch knowing she would die alone.

I'm so sorry, Harry says. I—

Eddie pulls out a small revolver and cocks it. A name. Say anything else and you die. I'll find out anyway. You might as well save your life.

Kevin.

See. That wasn't so hard, was it?

He was pulled over for driving under the influence just a few miles further down the same road, but instead of taking him in, the deputy, a member of my parish, called me. He didn't know he'd hit anyone.

When Kevin regains consciousness, he's lying on the side of the highway not far from the Stump Hole, his head throbbing, his vision blurred.

A favorite local swimming site for teens, the Stump Hole is a brackish inlet in the bay filled with bald cypress trees—both living and dead, logs and root systems.

As he tries to sit up, the dull throb transforms into a screaming sharp stab, and the earth beneath him spins so rapidly he gets motion sick and vomits.

How had he gotten here? He has no idea. He'd been getting into his small truck and . . .

He didn't remember driving, but looks around to see if he's had an accident. His truck is nowhere around, wrecked or otherwise. In fact, nothing is.

He's completely alone on the side of the highway in the darkness.

He's sure Kevin's head aches a bit, but it's nothing compared to the pain he's about to experience, the pain Hope had felt in her last few horrific moments on the earth. Headlights off, parked several car lengths away, Eddie strains to see Kevin. As he waits for him to stand, he wonders if the blow to the back of his head had been too hard.

In the passenger's seat of the idling car, beneath a penlight that illuminates a single strip, lies the tattered copies of the accident report, including the highway patrolman's diagram, now a blueprint for revenge so symmetrical it's scientific.

Eventually, slowly, Kevin stands and begins to wobble down the side of the highway.

As Eddie shifts the car into drive and begin to ease into position, he pictures Hope shivering in the cold, alone, scared, risking all for love, making the grand romantic gesture her dad seemed to think was so important.

His little girl—the one who nursed every stray animal that passed their way, the one who could never think of anything she wanted for Christmas or birthdays, the one who sat alone at junior high dances, the one so quiet and kind, so often overlooked. She had been too good for this world. He should have protected her better. He shouldn't have encouraged her to come over here on New Year's Eve. What was he thinking?

The truth was, he wanted her to change, to toughen up, become more outgoing, assertive. He was pushing her a bit because he was afraid she wouldn't make it in the real world if she didn't—

Oh, God, he says, and begins to cry. I'm sorry, honey. I'm so sorry.

When Kevin is near the place where he took Hope's life, Eddie punches the gas and speeds toward him, leaving his lights off. He wants Kevin to know what's coming, but he doesn't want to risk warning him too soon.

At the last possible moment, he switches on his brights. Kevin spins around, eyes wide and frightened, and in that split second the expression on his face reveals he knows what's coming.

As Eddie watches, searching for signs of recognition in Kevin's face, he sees something so odd it's humorous, or would be, if it weren't so pittiful, so futile—Kevin holds out his hands in a defensive gesture. Two tons of metal careening toward him and he raises his hands.

Had Hope done the same?

Crumpled as if there's no body inside his clothes, Kevin lays several feet off the highway, across a ditch, against the base of a thick pine tree.

Did you stop to check on her? Eddie asks.
Huh? Kevin manages in a confused, wet, airy voice.
Was she still alive? Did she say anything?
Help me.
Tell me.
Who? Kevin asks, his voice faint as if coming from a far-off place, most of it getting lost along the way. The girl you showed us?

Did she say anything?

How would *I* know?

You didn't even stop? Did you even know you hit her?

How did Harry get you to do this? Kevin asks. I wouldn't've told. It was just a . . . I just wanted him to do what he promised me.

I know you did it, Eddie says. The deputy confirmed it.

I got pulled over, Kevin says. But I didn't hit your daughter.

What?

Harry came and picked me up, he says. He'd been drinking.

Eddie's stomach churns, and he feels vomit rising up his throat.

What are you saying?

Tell him I wouldn't've told. Tell him I forgive him, he says. That I . . . don't . . . hold . . .

As Eddie falls back, waves of nausea rippling through him, he hears the sounds of sirens in the distance. A moment later, as the flashing lights strobe the disturbing scene, Eddie thinks, You just did the same thing Harry did. You killed an innocent. And yours wasn't an accident.

Beyond, the emergency vehicles, civilian cars stop. In the gathering crowd of bored townspeople, he sees Maria's tear-streaked face, as her warning echoes in his mind.

When you seek revenge, dig two graves.

She, like everything, is intermittently illuminated in bursts of red—like the flashes of an unheeded caution light on an empty road in the middle of a moonless night.

Death of a Desperate Woman

Get you guys anything else? Maria asked.

Lefty, Harry, and RD shook their heads.

Midmorning on a Tuesday at the Desperation Diner, the breakfast crowd long since left for work, the lunch crowd not yet made it in. Maria's boys were still in the large U-shaped booth in the front corner, table cleared, only their coffee cups remaining.

Only five white-haired men, all in their late sixties, all wrinkled and irrelevant, had the distinction of being Maria's boys. Jerry, a retiree from the electrical cooperative, was the most talkative and the biggest flirt. Tall, thin, soft-spoken, Sid, said the least. A recent widower, she worried about him the most.

The old-fashioned diner was bright, the greenish glow from the many florescents overhead mixing with the orange-tinted sunlight streaming in the plate glass windows in the front. Above soiled, worn industrial green carpet, ripped orange leatherette booths surrounded chipped Formica tables.

A lap dance, Jerry said.

Maria's head snapped around toward him, her straight blond hair whipping around to smack the clear complexion of her flawless face.

What'd I tell you? she said. No ordering off menu. And if you think your heart can stand it, you can get a lap dance in about ten hours over at Tan Fannies.

Why don't you work there? he asked.

Tits're too small, ass is too white, she said.

As she had expected, her boys were shocked to hear such language coming from their Maria. Gasps, whistles, and grunts accompanied wide eyes that immediately darted to her tits and ass.

Maria Bella had been serving coffee and bacon and eggs and hamburgers and key lime pie at the Desperation Diner for over five years now, was liked by everyone, adored by her regulars—the older men who met daily for leisurely meals, unrushed conversation, and a bit of flirting with the beautiful Bella—but she was still an outsider, a stranger in a strange land and always would be. And that was the way she wanted it.

God, I love it when you talk dirty, Jerry said.

Beneath Maria's big brown eyes, her perfect white teeth peaked out from a repressed smile.

That's almost as good as a lap dance, Lefty said.

Better, Harry said. I've gotta rush home and change my Depends.

Part of what would forever keep Maria an outsider was her mystique, the way she just showed up in town one day, took a waitressing job in the diner, rented a vacant house trailer in Villa Hermosa, and kept to herself, spending her free time at the Desperation Public Library or the AA meeting in the musty meeting hall of the Episcopal church.

You've got plenty to work with, RD said. You look about a billion times better than the best Tan Fannies has ever had.

Ah, that's so sweet, she said.

She looked over at Sid for a response, but he didn't say anything. He was smiling, which was an improvement, and for an instant there seemed to be the hint of a twinkle in his eye.

Jerry said, Why couldn't you've gotten a job at Tan Fannies back when you first so mysteriously appeared in our little town? You'd've made a hell of a lot more money than working here. Tits always outdo tips.

What *did* bring you to Casablanca? Sid asked.

Maria's full resplendent smile was as breathtaking as it was unexpected.

My health, she said. I came for the waters.

The whole town wondered where Maria came from and what had brought her to Desperation. Her boys made a game of guessing, each continually searching for new and clever ways to ask the young woman who seemed to have read every great book and memorized every good line from every great movie.

Waters? What waters? Sid asked. We're in the desert.

Sid's lost his mind, Jerry said to the others. Losing Gwen was just too much on him.

Sid, Left said loudly. We're in Florida. There's water everywhere.

We're repeating lines from one of the best films ever made, Maria said.

Oh, RD said. The old Bogart movie. What's the name of—

Jerry turned to him, exasperation on his face. He just said it. *Casablanca.*

Did he? I missed it.

Over near the tall glass case of homemade deserts, two businessmen were growing weary of waiting to be seated. Maria knew it, could sense it in their body language, but didn't rush this, her favorite part of the job.

I've often speculated on why you don't return to where you came from, Sid said. Did you abscond with church funds? Did you run off with a senator's daughter? I'd like to think you killed a man. It's the romantic in me.

Even though she knew the line, knew what was coming, a twitch at killed a man gave her away. She could never be a poker player, Sid thought, but she's a killer. He knew that now. What he didn't know was what he was going to do about it.

She killed someone, Sid said.

Huh?

He and Lefty were shuffling down Main Street on their way to the post office. The stores on either side of the street were open for business, there just wasn't any.

Maria. She's hiding here because she killed a man—or a woman.

RD's not the only one who's lost his goddam mind.

Next to Sid, Lefty looked even shorter than he was, his rounded, slightly hunched shoulders taking away even further from his already diminutive stature.

I never would've used the *Casablanca* line if I thought she had really killed someone.

Maria's not a murderer, Lefty said.

She is. I saw it in her eyes.

I've known a few in my time.

What? Sid asked.

Killers. Maria ain't one.

Though no one knew for sure exactly, Lefty was rumored to have worked for the mob. Whether as a bagman or an enforcer, he had seen many more murderers than Sid as a State Farm insurance agent.

She is. I'm telling you.

So what if she is?

Well, Sid said, then paused a moment, I don't know.

They padded along in silence for a while, raising their swollen and misshapen hands to passing cars, nodding to approaching pedestrians.

I want you to find out who she is and where she came from, Sid said.

Lefty shook his head.

I know you know people, Sid said.

If I ever knew people—and I'm saying *if*, they're all dead by now.

Come on, Left, Sid said. What've I ever asked of you?

I don't know, Sid, Lefty said, shaking his head. Why you wanna know?

Just curious. And bored. Nothing better to do.

Whatta you gonna *do* with the information? I don't wanna see Maria get jammed up. I like her.

Nothing. I swear. I'm just dying to know.

On a clear September day in 2001, Maria Bella ended the life of Nancy Most. It had been a long time ago now, but in her memory it would always be as if it had just happened. She hadn't intended to do it, didn't even know she was going to the moment before she did it. No one could argue premeditation. And no one ever would. No one in the small coastal town of Desperation in north Florida even knew who Nancy Most was, and as far as Maria knew, no one was looking for her—not in Desperation, and not as Maria Bella.

Life could be so random. One morning, Nancy Most was working her mall job at Ann Taylor Loft, going about her life, unaware how little of it there was left, and by lunch she was dead. She was an addict, a user in every sense of the word, a woman who traded on her good looks and hot body to get what she wanted. She had hurt too many people, but did she deserve to die? Maria Bella thought so. Fate had left the decision up to her, and she had chosen. Since then, she had thought about it often—nearly every day—but she didn't regret what she had done. Given the same circumstances, she'd do it again.

Lunch on a Thursday, and Maria's boys were in their booth. Sid still looked at her funny—though only when she wasn't looking—but the others seemed just the same.

When RD finished his burger, only the onions he removed from it were left on his plate. Jerry slid the plate over in front of him as Maria returned to the table. Looking from the plate of onions to her, he raised his eyebrows and wondered if he had given her enough to work with.

She smiled. There was one scene you *did* write.

About the onions? Jerry asked.

He was obviously pleased with himself. The others turned their attention to them, attempting to figure out what book or movie was being quoted from.

Yes.

Does Henry mind onions? Jerry asked.

I know this, Sid said. Henry. Henry. Who is—

Yes, Maria said. He can't bear them. Do you like them?

Yes, Jerry said. Is it possible to fall in love over a dish of onions?

Very good, Jerry, Maria said, and rewarded him with a small smile.

You're the one to be commended, he said.

I know I know this, Sid said, looking at Jerry. Is it a movie or a book?

Both, he said.

Actually, it's a scene from a movie in a book and in the movie based on the book, Maria said.

That doesn't make any—

The End of the Affair, Sid said, snapping his arthritic fingers.

Very good, Maria said.

He didn't look at her—still hadn't since he saw the confession her eyes had made.

Better than *Casablanca*, Jerry said.

How old you think Maria is? Lefty asked.

Sid shrugged.

Lingering after the others had gone, the two elderly gentlemen with nowhere to be were standing out on the sidewalk in front of the diner, watching Maria Bella through the enormous plate glass window.

Probably younger than she looks. There's something in her eyes. I'd say she's had some hard years. Mid-thirties?

Eighty-four.

I was wrong, she's aged well, Sid said. Damn well.

The two men were silent a moment. When Lefty didn't say anything else, Sid said, Seriously.

I'm serious.

Left, that beautiful young woman in there is not eighty-four.

Maybe not, but the woman whose identity she stole is, Lefty said. Or would be if she weren't dead.

She killed an old woman and took her identity?

All I know for sure is Maria Bella lived most of her life on the Outer Banks, taught school, ran one of those little lighthouse gift shops, Lefty said. During the months leading up to her death, she had a live-in companion who helped with cooking and cleaning and offered her some much needed company—a pretty blond girl who appeared out of nowhere to apply for the job.

How long ago was that?

Just before she showed up here.

Where was she before she came to live with the real Maria Bella?

Should know in another day or so.

Sid nodded, staring at the woman he had thought of as Maria Bella for the past few years.

You're just curious, right, Sid? Not gonna do anything about it—no matter what we find out.

Right. Just want to know.

Then stop staring like you're at a goddam zoo.

Why won't you look at me? Maria asked.

Sid made eye contact with her for the first time in several days. I look at you, he said. I'm looking at you right now.

They had encountered one another in the small, dimly lit Desperation Public Library, and were now seated at a round wooden table near the fiction section. On the table in front of Maria two stacks of reference books blocked Sid's view of the legal pad she had been making notes on when he past by and she looked up, saw him, and insisted that he join her.

You know what I mean, she said. Ever since you saw my reaction to the line you quoted from *Casablanca*, you look at me differently.

Sid didn't say anything.

Like the pitiful collection it held, the Desperation Public Library was old and had not been well cared for; its dusty books sat on sagging shelves beneath flickering florescent lights.

Eventually, Sid said, What are you researching?

Just something for a little project I'm working on, she said.

A project?

It's nothing, really.

He squinted to make out the titles on the spines of the books across the table from him. He made out *Crime Scene Investigation* and *Arson* something another.

I'm not who you think I am, she said.

How do you know what I think?

And even if I've done horrible things in the past, she said, isn't it who I am now that counts?

Sid nodded, but there was no conviction in the gesture.

Don't people deserve a second chance? she asked. Don't we all need one from time to time?

We do.

I've changed, she said. I'm not the person I was, and I'll never be again. Can't that be enough? Can't you just accept me for who I am now?

I just want to know your story, he said.

You know it, she said. It began when I got here.

Then your back story, he said.

Why? she asked. Why does it matter?

He shrugged.

I walked out of one life and into another, she said. Can't we just leave it at that?

Okay, he said, but it wasn't very convincing.

I want you to read something, she said, standing up and walking over to a shelf about halfway down a nearby aisle. Ever heard of the Flitcraft Parable?

He shook his head.

She returned to the table with an old musty, misshapen copy of Dashiell Hammett's *The Maltese Falcon*, opened it to Chapter Seven, laid it on the table in front of him, and turned and walked away.

He began to read.

A man named Flitcraft had left his real-estate-office, in Tacoma, to go to luncheon one day and had never returned. He did not keep an engagement to play golf after four that afternoon, though he had taken the initiative in making the engagement less than half an hour before he went out to luncheon. His wife and children never saw him again. His wife and he were supposed to be on the best of terms. He had two children, boys, one five and the other three. He owned his house in a Tacoma suburb, a new Packard, and the rest of the appurtenances of successful American living.

He went like that, Spade said, like a fist when you open your hand. Well, that was in 1922. In 1927 I was with one of the big detective agencies in Seattle. Mrs. Flitcraft came in and told us somebody had seen a man in Spokane who looked a lot like her husband. I went over there. It was Flitcraft, all right. He had been living in Spokane for a couple of years as Charles—that was his first name—Pierce. He had a automobile-business that was netting him twenty or twenty-five thousand a year, a wife, a baby son, owned his home in a Spokane suburb, and usually got away to play golf after four in the afternoon during the season.

Here's what happened to him. Going to lunch he passed an office building that was being put up—just the skeleton. A beam or something fell eight or ten stories down and smacked the sidewalk alongside him. It brushed pretty close to him, but didn't touch him, though a piece of the sidewalk was chipped off and flew up and hit his cheek. It only took a piece of skin off, but he still had the scar when I saw him. He rubbed it with his finger—well, affectionately—when he told me about it. He was scared stiff of course, he said, but he was more shocked than really frightened. He felt like somebody had taken the lid off life and let him look at the works.

Flitcraft had been a good citizen and a good husband and father, not by any outer compulsion, but simply because he was a man most comfortable in step with his surroundings. He had been raised that way. The people he knew were like that. The life he knew was a clean, orderly, sane, responsible affair. Now a falling beam had shown him that life was fundamentally none of these things. He, the good citizen-husband-father, could be wiped out between office and restaurant by the accident of a falling beam. He knew then that men died at haphazard like that, and lived only while blind chance spared them.

It was not, primarily, the injustice of it that disturbed him: he accepted that after the first shock. What disturbed him was the discovery that in sensibly ordering his affairs he had got out of step, and not in step, with life. He said he knew before he had gone twenty feet from the fallen beam that he would never know peace until he had adjusted himself to this new glimpse of life. By the time he had eaten his luncheon he had found his means of adjustment. Life could be ended for him at random by a falling beam: He would change his life at random by simply going away.

He went to Seattle that afternoon, Spade said, and from there by boat to San Francisco. For a couple of years he wandered around and then drifted back to the Northwest, and settled in Spokane and got married. His second wife didn't look like the first, but they were more alike than they were different. You know, the kind of women that play fair games of golf and bridge and like new salad recipes. He wasn't sorry for what he had done. It seemed reasonable enough to him. I don't think he even knew he had settled back naturally in the same groove he had jumped out of in Tacoma. But that the part of it I always liked. He adjusted himself to beams falling, and then no more of them fell, and he adjusted himself to them not falling.

So what's it mean? Lefty asked.

That she walked away from her life and started a new one, Sid said. She's been born again, but not because of a beam nearly falling on her. Because she killed someone.

It was early morning. The two men were lingering out in front of the diner on their way to join the others for breakfast.

I don't know, Sid, he said. That's a bit of a stretch.

What else did you find out?

Not much, Lefty said. It's as if she didn't exist before she moved in with old Mrs. Bella.

See, Sid said. Like Flitcraft.

I guess.

Anything else?

She sends anonymous sympathy cards to Alfred and Angie Most up in New York and has flowers put on their daughter Nancy's grave. She also gets checks from the William Morris Agency at a PO box under the name of Nancy Lost.

She feels bad for killing their daughter, but not bad enough not to use a variation of her name, Sid said. What are the checks for?

TV scripts, Lefty said. She writes for some chick network.

Just then the fire whistle from the station on Second Street started to blow, and the two men turned to see blackish-gray smoke rising from Villa Hermosa.

Jerry and the others came out the front door.

That's Maria's place, RD said.

She coming? Lefty asked. We can walk down there with her.

She didn't show up for work today, Jerry said. Come on.

Sid looked at Lefty, their eyes locking in a moment of realization.

As the five bent and limping men hobbled toward Villa Hermosa, all Sid could think about were the research books stacked in front of Maria on the library table.

By the time the men arrived, the rental trailer was a melted mass of charred, wet materials. What was left of the walls and roof were flat on the floor now.

Never seen one go that fast, Nate, a volunteer fireman, said.

Had to have some help, Coy, the oldest of the fireman, said. I've been doing this a long time. Nothing burns that fast without some kind of accelerant—not even a mobile home.

Was Maria inside? Jerry asked.

Huh?

The two firemen were unaware of the old men behind them.

Was there anyone inside, goddam it? Jerry yelled.

Hey, back off, old man, Nate said. We don't know anything yet. Y'all need to back away from this area.

GOT SOMETHING, a fireman yelled from the back of what used to be the trailer.

What is it? RD asked.

We can't see any better than you can, Jerry said. Just wait a minute.

Let's move around back for a better look, Harry said.

They did, making a wide circle around the trucks and coming up in between two other trailers, but when they saw the blackened body, nearly skeletal now, they wished they hadn't.

Oh God, RD said, turning quickly and losing the little breakfast he had eaten.

Who the fuck would do this to that sweet girl? Jerry said.

Sid leaned over and whispered in Lefty's ear, Who'd that sweet girl do this to.

Lefty turned and looked at him for a long moment, then jerked his head, motioning him away from the others.

What did you do? Lefty asked when they were far enough away so the others couldn't overhear them.

You think I did this?

Lefty shook his head. I don't mean the fire. What'd you say to her?

Nothing.

You said you were just curious. You wouldn't do anything.

I didn't.

What'd you say to her? Lefty asked again. You had to push her, couldn't just leave it alone, had to let her know we were on to her, and now she's killed again and disappeared. Whoever that is in there, Lefty added, jerking his head toward the remains of the trailer, you're an accessory to her murder.

When Sid's eyes opened in the middle of the night, heart pounding, mind racing, he knew he was not alone in his dark bedroom.

Maria? Sid said.

Leave the light off, she said.

Sid wondered if he were about to die, and he realized he really didn't mind all that much.

You here to kill me?

To ask a favor.

Really? he asked, the high-pitched surprise clearing the sleepiness out of his voice.

Don't try to find me, she said. I'm leaving tonight. Disappearing again. And it would just be nice not to be followed.

I'm an old man, he said. I won't be following anybody.

I mean don't have it done, she said.

The police won't know that's not me in the trailer, she said. Just don't tell them any differently.

Who is it? he asked. Who'd you kill so you could escape?

I didn't kill anyone, she said. I swear. I wouldn't expect you to keep quiet about murder. I dug up a recently buried body.

My Gwen?

NO, she said. God, no. I would never. Anyway, this woman was already dead. All I did was dig her up and burn her body. That's awful, but necessary—and nowhere close to murder.

Won't the police know it's not you?

I burned the body before I lit the trailer so it'd be unrecognizable, she said, and no one knows me. I haven't left any evidence.

Guess you're getting pretty good at this by now, he said.

What's that mean?

Maria Bella.

Yeah?

I meant the real Maria Bella, he said. You killed her.

No, I didn't, she said. She was an old lady and died a natural death. I took her identity, but that's all. I can't believe you know about that.

Tell me about Nancy Most, he said.

A long silence followed his request.

She was a coke head, she said. Strung out most of the time. You can't imagine the things she did.

Tell me.

She hurt her parents so much they finally cut her loose, she said. They loved her, were so patient, but . . .

She trailed off and they were silent a moment.

I can't believe you know about her, she said.

What do you write in those cards you send her parents?

Lies, she said. I tell them their daughter changed before she died, that they would be so proud, but she didn't. She'd do okay for a little while. Get cleaned up, get a job, get a man, but it wasn't long before she'd be right back on the shit. The last time she got cleaned up, she got a job at the Ann Taylor Loft store in the concourse mall at the World Trade Center. She did fine for a while, but was already headed back down when the planes flew into the towers on 9-11. You know what she did when the planes hit? Locked up her store and started up Tower I to see her supplier. Imagine. The world's falling down around her, and all she can think about is securing her next fix. She would have been in the tower when it came down if a cop hadn't grabbed her in the stairwell and forced her out.

Sid's mind was working. The woman in the room with him must have had a brother or a dad who was cop or a fireman or a worker who got killed because of Nancy Most.

She got out?

Before the tower came down? Yeah. Not everyone who died that day was killed by terrorists.

She was a drug addict, but why'd she have to die? Sid asked. What'd she do?

Did you not hear me? she said. She was never going to change. She got pregnant one time. If that didn't clean her up, nothing would. When she delivered, her little premature, underweight baby had withdrawals. You know what she did? Gave it up for adoption and kept on shoving shit up her nose.

Sid didn't say anything.

Will you give me your word as a gentleman you won't tell the cops or try to find me?

How can I not report you? he asked. Even if I believe you about the victim in the trailer and the real Maria Bella, you murdered Nancy Most.

I wouldn't call it murder.

There's got to be more to it than that she was a drug addict, he said. You don't go around killing drug addicts. What did Nancy do to you?

What? she asked, sounding genuinely perplexed.

You didn't just kill her because she was a drug addict, he said. Why?

I don't understand, she said. I thought you knew. You knew everything else. I didn't literally kill Nancy. I just let people think she was in the building when it came down.

But she wasn't, he said. So what happened to her?

Flitcraft, remember? she said. Nancy walked out of the building and when she saw it come down, when she realized how many thousands of people who didn't deserve to die were killed and that she was spared, she kept on walking. She walked out of her life and never looked back. I buried Nancy Most on

September 11, 2001, and was born again—eventually as Maria Bella. Today, I buried Maria Bella. Soon, I'll be someone else. But I'll never look back, never go back to being Nancy Most, a worthless addict who didn't deserve to live—not when so many who should be alive aren't.

Go ahead, Nancy—

Don't call me that, she said. Nancy's dead.

Go ahead, Maria or whoever you are now, he said. I won't follow you. I won't tell anyone. I'll miss you. I'm sorry I didn't just leave it all alone.

Goodbye, Sid, she said. I'll miss you, too.

Write me sometime, he said, but there was no reply. Nancy Most/Maria Bella/Joan Doe was already out of the room, out of his life for good.

Acknowledgements

Special thanks to Pam, Lynn, Jim, Adam, and Jeanmarie.

About the Author

Michael Lister is a novelist, essayist, playwright, and screenwriter. He lives in North Florida. His website is www.MichaelLister.com